Kiss Me, Tate

LOVE IN RUSTIC WOODS

KAREN CANTWELL

ACKNOWLEDGMENTS

Special thanks go to the many people who have helped see this book to publication: Beth Balberchak and Misha Crews for their beta and proofreading; my family for putting up with me when I get a little stressed; the wonderful people at Streetlight Graphics for doing so much in a short amount of time; and last, but most importantly, to Maria E. Schneider, my friend and editor who worked tirelessly on such a tight deadline. You're the greatest, Maria!

"I see a woman may be made a fool, if she had not a spirit to resist."
—William Shakespeare, *Taming of the Shrew*

CHAPTER ONE

UNNY BERGEN'S GREATEST WEAKNESS WAS her inability to see past people's social veneers. Which was why she found herself standing with a cardboard box tucked under one arm and a severance check in her other hand, wondering what the heck had just happened.

She'd been fired. Or rather, "let go" as Dr. Page, DDS, had said. He claimed he couldn't afford her, but that was plain crazy. He barely paid her above minimum wage for a receptionist position that required far more than simply answering a phone, for crying out loud. And she was the *only* receptionist, which meant he'd need to find someone else for less pay pretty darn quick. No, it didn't add up. Bunny might be naive, but she wasn't stupid.

As she balanced the box filled with personal items and dug for her car keys in her purse, Lois, the senior dental technician, hurried down the front walk of the Rustic Woods Medical Building. She stopped in front of Bunny, putting a fist to her hip. "He did it, huh?" The woman, easily ten years Bunny's senior, looked at her watch. "What did he do, call you in early to give you the boot?"

Bunny nodded, the memory of her termination episode knotting her stomach. "You knew?"

"Let's just say that I overheard some things."

"What things?"

"Remember yesterday, when Broom Hildie was in?"

Bunny deepened her frown. She didn't care for the nickname the staff had given Dr. Page's wife. It seemed awfully harsh given that the woman appeared perfectly cordial. Yet during her short, three-week stint at the dental practice, the technicians had shared rants more than once about 'Broom Hildie' Page. She thought back to the previous day and Mrs. Page's lunchtime visit. She had smiled and shaken Bunny's hand, introducing herself. Said how glad she was to meet her and that Dr. Page had mentioned many times how lucky he was to find someone as hard working and dedicated as Bunny. Nothing had seemed out of the ordinary to Bunny. She shook her head. "I don't get it. She was nice. I was nice. What did I miss?"

"She had an apoplectic fit outside when they left for lunch. She didn't even wait to get to their car before she tore into him."

"About what?"

"Your boobs."

"What?" Bunny covered her chest instinctively, mortified.

"Said they were hanging out like you were having a two-for-one sale."

"They were not!" Bunny dipped her gaze and examined the guilty parties. It was true, she didn't try to hide them. She preferred blouses that complemented the cleavage she inherited from Nana McDougal, but she sure as heck didn't let them "hang out." Plenty of respectable women wore flattering clothes. The accusation caused her face to flame.

"It gets worse," Lois said.

Bunny didn't know if she wanted to hear anything worse. Lois told her anyway. "She called you a skank."

The word hit Bunny like a punch to the stomach, making her nauseous. She'd been the subject of nasty rumors before, passed on by people who didn't know her. People who judged her simply because she was attractive and chose to wear decidedly feminine attire. She didn't need this kind of trauma in her life again. Taking a moment to steady her rage and fantasizing about punching Hildie Page in her puffed up, collagen-filled lips, she pressed her car fob and heard it unlock. With some clumsy maneuverings, she pried the door open and shoved the box into the back seat. Slamming the door loudly helped her vent some of the indignation, but certainly not all of it.

Lois pulled something from her coat pocket. "Here." She handed a folded piece of blue paper to Bunny. "I thought this might happen, and I know you need the work. They need a receptionist at the Nature Center, and they're interviewing today. You should probably get over there as soon as possible."

Bunny took the paper with shaking hands.

"I'm sorry," Lois said. "I know it hurts, but I thought you should know."

Tears welled in Bunny's eyes, but she fought them back. "It's..." she gulped, not wanting Lois to see her break down. "It's fine." She waved the blue paper in the air while opening the driver's side door. "Thank you for this."

Seated in her car with the heat running, Bunny pondered her dilemma. She should sue. Surely you couldn't fire a person based on her neckline or on ridiculous lies spread by cranky wives. Waterworks began flowing at the thought. She would have to hire a lawyer, and lawyer's fees were the reason she'd taken this ridiculously low-paying job in the first place. Fighting her ex-husband for custody of her two boys had nearly bankrupted her.

After allowing herself a ten-Kleenex cry in her twenty-year-old, junk-yard-ready Ford, Bunny unfolded the paper and inspected it more carefully. Lois' scrawl was nearly indecipherable, which didn't matter, really. If she decided to rush over, red-rimmed eyes and all, she certainly knew her way to the Nature Center. Most people in Rustic Woods did, especially if they had children. Her own boys had attended summer camps and boy scout nature hikes there.

The question was, did she want to interview for the position at all? She didn't have a resume with her or anything. Not that there was anything on the resume. The job with Dr. Page was her first real work experience outside of a summer internship with a fashion magazine between her junior and senior years in college. Not exactly a Nature Center sort of a background. And, technically, now she'd have to add her three-week stint at Dr. Page's that ended in termination. Her cheeks cramped and water filled her eyes again. She yanked three more tissues from the box, grabbed her phone and dialed Barb for advice.

Her friend picked up on the third ring, and Bunny started blubbering again, even before she could hear the "Hello."

"Bunny, what's wrong? Has something happened?" Barb asked.

Barbara Marr lived one street over from Bunny and was a rock as far as Bunny was concerned. They'd become friends during a very strange time in Bunny's life, and the fact that Barb had tried to shoot her in the foot only increased her admiration for the woman. Barb had pulled the trigger to save Bunny's life, after all.

Bunny choked back sobs. "He fired me."

"The dentist? Why?"

"My cleavage, apparently."

"This sounds like a discussion we should have over a glass of wine."

Bunny laughed over a sniffle. "It's nine o'clock in the morning, Barb."

"Coffee then. Do you want to come over?"

"I don't know. One of the dental technicians told me about another job, but I need to go over right now."

"Another dentist office?"

"No. The Nature Center."

"That's great!"

"You think?"

"I do. You need a pep talk? I can meet you there."

Bunny sniffled some more. She didn't deserve a friend as sweet as Barb. "Thanks. Can you bring—"

"Getting a turtleneck from my closet right now," Barb told her. "And a sweater for good measure."

Barb's white minivan was already parked in the large graveled parking lot of the Rustic Woods Nature Center when Bunny pulled in, her cranky old car coughing and sputtering as she turned off the ignition.

They met between the two cars. The curly-haired woman gave Bunny a tight hug that really did make her feel much better. "Thank you for coming. I'm still not sure about this, though."

"Pshaw," said Barb. "You'll go in there and wow their socks off. They'll love you. Probably hire you on the spot. Now let's get you interview-ready."

Bunny looked around. "Where?"

Barb tugged hard to open the sliding van door. "My van. Hop in the back."

Bunny, despite her name, didn't hop anywhere easily. She was a tall woman with some fairly long and lanky bones.

Grinning, Barb handed her an emerald green turtleneck. "Green to match your eyes. No one will even notice your knockers. Speaking of which, you owe me a story while you're dressing."

Doubtfully, Bunny wrangled herself into the back while trying to keep her black skirt from shimmying too high or her heels from flipping off her feet. Once inside, she breathed heavily, winded from the work-out involved. When spring arrived, she needed to put some serious effort into a plan for more exercise.

Barb followed, slid the door closed, and scanned the parking lot through tinted windows. "I think you're safe. Undress, and I'll keep lookout."

Bunny unbuttoned her blouse while recounting her tale of woe, but grunted the story out less easily while trying to work her way into her friend's turtleneck. Once she had one arm halfway on, she knew she was in trouble. It was tight. Very tight. "Lois said she called me a skank," she said, more or less finishing her story. "What size is this?"

"Medium. A skank? Based on what?"

"I don't know." Bunny contorted this way and that, attempting to get the thing over her head and down over her bodice. "Medium, huh?"

"What size do you usually wear?"

"Not a medium." Bunny pulled and yanked and shimmied. Finally, she had the turtleneck in place. Well, sort of. She looked down.

"Uh-oh," said Barb.

Uh-oh was right. Donning a too-small top had the opposite of her intended effect. Instead of diminishing the large appearance of her chest, the constrictive fabric accentuated her upper girth. Her hopes sank. "I have a broad back."

"To match your broad front," said Barb with a light chuckle. "I'm so jealous. The only time I ever had cleavage was when I was breastfeeding. I took pictures so I could look back and remember the good days." She shook her head while Bunny laughed, thankful for her friend's dry humor.

"Back to the drawing board on Project Hide and No Peek," Barb said with a sigh. "Get your blouse back on. We'll have to cover you with this sweater." Barb gave another scan to make sure the coast was clear for Bunny to strip.

Back outside, they battle-planned the wearing of the sweater, which was also on the small side for Bunny, but not nearly as disastrous as the turtleneck. Bunny suggested wearing her winter coat into the interview. "I could say, I don't know, that I was feeling a fever coming on."

They killed that idea almost immediately. Not only would the coat make Bunny appear odd, but the interviewer might get distracted worrying about germs in the air instead of paying attention to Bunny's qualifications.

Bunny fiddled with the sweater some more, then decided she'd done enough. Either she'd get this job or she wouldn't. She needed to just get in there, get it done, and get out.

She took a deep breath. "I'm ready."

"That's the spirit." Barb gave her a warm smile and took Bunny by the shoulders. "Remember, you're a brave, strong, confident woman."

"I'm not that confident..."

"What did you just say?"

"Confident. I'm a confident woman."

"So confident, they'll have no choice but to give you that job, right here, right now. Do you want me to come in with you?"

Bunny's first thought was, *Yes please. In fact, can you interview in my place?* But she dug down deep and found some courage. She shook her head. "No. No. I'm good."

"Do you want me to wait?"

"I don't know how long I'll be. You should go home. Can I come by after?"

"Sure. I'll have coffee waiting."

"Have that wine chilled just in case."

Bunny stepped into the Rustic Woods Nature Center and not-so-confidently peeked around the quiet place for a person to consult about this possible receptionist position. To her right and left were rooms with posters on the walls and terrariums containing local plant life and probably a snake or two. Was there a reception desk? She couldn't remember. If they needed a receptionist, there must be a reception desk. Her heels clacked on the hardwood floor as she proceeded tentatively forward, her head leading the rest of her shaky body.

"Hello?" She clacked a few more steps ahead. "Hello?"

Aha. There it was. Halfway down the main hallway, she saw the appropriately rustic wooden reception desk. Seated there was a girl who looked only a year or two older than her son Charlie. Bunny wondered why the girl didn't answer. A few more loud steps, and Bunny could see the reason why. The girl was reading a book and had tuned the world out with ear buds and an MP3 player.

Bunny clattered a little more boldly to the desk. A teenager wasn't so threatening. She could handle that. The girl still hadn't noticed her even though Bunny stood right in front of her now. Bunny cleared her throat. No reaction.

"Tap her book. She's oblivious." The low male voice came from behind Bunny and startled her enough to make her jump.

A man and a woman sat on a bench against the wall. The man was dressed like he'd just come from a shift at an auto mechanic shop. The woman, a brunette, was younger and interview-ready in a salmon suit which, while attractive in a sort of Floridian way, seemed to Bunny to be entirely out of place in the month of February, even if March was just a few days away. She gripped a soft leather briefcase in her lap, as if afraid the man next to her might steal it.

"Tap the book," the man repeated. "That's what I did."

Bunny smiled hesitantly at the grimy man. She reached out, giving the girl's book a small poke with her index finger.

Rather than seeming startled, the girl raised her eyes with an annoyed glare. After what felt like years to Bunny, the little brat pulled one bud from her ear. "Can I help you?"

"I was told...I mean, I'd like to..."

The girl sighed while Bunny fumbled to speak her thoughts coherently. The sigh irritated Bunny, prodding her to get a grip on her wits. "The receptionist position," she said with more certainty. "I want to interview."

"What's your name?"

"Bu—" She stopped herself just in time. When interviewing, she always used her legal name, Robin. It sounded more adult, she thought. More professional. "Robin Bergen."

The girl made a grand gesture of leaning over to look at a clipboard. She scanned the thing for all of a half a second, then lifted her eyes to Bunny, acting very bored about the whole process. "You're not on the list."

"That's okay. I was told if I came right over, I could interview. I have a name..." she pulled the paper from her pocket. "I'm not sure what it is, though. Allison, maybe?"

The girl stared at Bunny. Bunny stared at the girl. A big clock on the wall made of redwood ticked and tocked. The unblinking girl tapped her finger once, twice, three times. "Or maybe it was Avril," Bunny finally said, her confidence waning. "I couldn't read her writing." She held the blue paper up for the girl to read, but the imp didn't seem interested. Without taking her accusing eyes off

Bunny, she picked up the phone and punched a button. "Abigail?" she said into the receiver.

Bunny heard a beeping noise, and a moment later a woman's voice sounded over the intercom. "Yes, Corinne?"

"Woman named Robin here was told she could just show up for an interview. What do I do?"

"She's not on the list?"

"Nope."

Afraid her chances at the job were slipping away, Bunny waved her hand in front of the girl's face. "Bunny Bergen. She might know that name. My friend Lois told me to come."

The girl emitted a sigh with so much force that papers on the desk fluttered. "Now she says her name is Bunny Bergen."

"Oh, for crying out loud, have her fill out an application. We'll see her at the end if we have time."

Bunny thanked the ill-mannered receptionist, plucked the offered application from her hand before it could be rescinded, and took the only space left on the bench. She tightened her grip on the pen and focused on making herself look good on paper.

The briefcase-clutching lady in the salmon suit was called in after a keenly dressed, well-manicured man exited from a door labeled *Conference Room*. The man had a wide smile on his face. *Must have gone well. Darn.* Bunny's nerves were beginning to affect her stomach. It twisted and turned and gurgled. Quite audibly.

Time seemed to creep by at a horrifically slow pace. Bunny looked at the clock on the wall for the hundredth time. It was dangerously close to noon. Would they have time for her? Finally, the grimy-looking man came through the door and motioned to her with one hand. "They said you can go in."

"Oh, thank you." Bunny rose, gathered her things, made sure the sweater wrapped nicely over her bosom, and teetered forward.

She had to pass through two sets of heavy wooden doors before entering the space that seemed to be less room and more conference table. And who were all of these people? Bunny had envisioned a one-on-one interview, much like the easy going time with Dr. Page, who had kindly put her at ease almost instantly. Here, at the horribly long table, sat five people. Five. They stared at her. Three men, two women. None of them smiled.

"I'm, um...sorry," Bunny stumbled. "I think I'm in the wrong place."

One of the women, one with scary hair and a scowl, spoke up. "Are you applying for the receptionist position or aren't you?"

"Oh, yes." Bunny held up the completed application. Her nerves were so frazzled, she feared she might faint. *I should have skipped this and gone straight to Barb's for that wine.*

The frizzy-haired woman raised a hand, indicating that Bunny should bring the application to her. While Bunny made the long walk to the back of the table, the woman made introductions. She pointed to the woman on her right—a short, round woman with glasses. "This is Olga, the Nature Center's Publicity and Outreach Coordinator. I'm Abigail, the Activities Coordinator." She pointed to a man next to her with a brown bushy mustache and even bushier eyebrows who looked like he belonged in a barbershop quartet. "This is Rupert Long, whom you may recognize—he's a member of the board of the Rustic Woods Association." Next in the lineup was a thin, pasty-faced man with a pointy nose. "That's George."

Bunny wondered why poor George didn't rate a designation. "And, finally," said Abigail, pointing to the man at the end of the line of interrogators. Bunny's eyes landed on the dark-haired, bearded man with the sleepy onyx eyes, a man who looked very familiar. Her heart fluttered when she realized why. No introduction was necessary. She knew the man. Not well, but she definitely knew him. He was back in town and, holy guacamole, he was more gorgeous than ever.

Elation quickly turned to agitation. *Crap*, she thought. *Why here? Why now? Now I'll really screw things up.*

Abigail's introduction continued, "This is—"

Bunny didn't mean to interrupt the woman. It just sort of happened. "I know Tate already," she said looking at the man. Her voice trembled slightly. "Nice to see you again."

Really, really nice.

CHAPTER TWO

*T*ATE KILBOURN WAS IRRITATED.

Why had George demanded that he sit in on the receptionist interviews? The position fell under Abigail's authority, not Tate's. As the Nature Center's lead naturalist, he was chin-high in work orders. Early winter storms had wreaked havoc throughout Rustic Woods, creating extra clean-up for his work crew. As if that wasn't enough, his father's health weighed on his mind.

One day, George would pay for wasting his time this way, but for now, Tate rebelled by refusing to engage in the process. While the other interviewers acted regal by asking ridiculously irrelevant questions, Tate reclined in his chair, occasionally rolling his eyes at the more inane utterances from the motley crew. The prospects were obviously all over-qualified. It was a receptionist position, for crying out loud. Yes, it was work—sometimes stressful when the phones started ringing off the hook in the spring—but nearly anyone could be trained for the job. Why were they talking to people with Masters Degrees in botany?

Finally, thought Tate, only one more hopeful candidate to snore through, and he was free. He was scrolling through emails on his cell phone, oblivious, when he realized

Abigail was about to introduce him. He shifted his gaze up and locked eyes with the final interviewee. While she was pleasing to look at, no one was more surprised than he was when the woman claimed to know him.

"I'm sorry," he said. "What did you say your name was?"

"Bunny." The woman brushed some hair behind one ear. "Bunny Bergen."

The name was familiar. He'd grown up in Rustic Woods, so it was possible that he did know her. He'd left when college called and hadn't returned until last year, so his memory for people and places was a little fuzzy. There had been a lot about the small Virginia suburb that he'd tried to forget.

"It says here," interrupted Abigail, "that your name is Robin."

"That's right." Bunny nodded vigorously. She pointed to a chair. "Can I sit? I'm a little...I mean, my feet..."

"Sit," Olga ordered abruptly in her thick Russian accent.

Tate suppressed a grin. Olga, bless her, came across very KGB.

The woman named Robin—who called herself Bunny—sat, and Tate leaned forward, more captivated than he'd been all day. She had a bit of a Marilyn Monroe-esque quality, which really didn't fit the Nature Center theme, but maybe that was a good thing. She might bring some fresh air to the stuffy seriousness that prevailed far too often around here. He motioned toward Abigail. "Can I see her application?" And while he waited for it to cross hands his way, he asked, "Bunny, do you have a resume?"

"Yeah. About that. I kind of rushed here because... um..." Bunny shook her head and pulled her unattractive wool sweater tighter around her as if she was trying to hide something. "No," she said. "Not with me. But I wrote everything down there. What you're looking at." Then her insides growled and moaned loudly enough for the whole room to hear. "Oh, my gosh," she said, tapping her middle. "Sorry about that. Hungry I guess. And nerves. I should really be honest—I'm a very honest and reliable person—this whole interviewing thing makes me very nervous."

Tate could tell Abigail wasn't impressed. Although, quite frankly, Abigail rarely looked impressed. The woman, who would be boss to the receptionist hired, started in. Her lips were pressed thin. "Let's just get down to the—"

"Can you answer phones, Bunny?" Tate interrupted.

Bunny looked from Abigail to Tate. The hope that shone on her face felt familiar. "Yes. Yes. I did that at Dr. Page's office." She offered a wide smile that Tate decided would be a nice change at the reception desk. Then it hit him. The smile. Suddenly he knew who she was.

"You had brown hair, right?"

She nodded. "You caught me. I bleach."

"You went to Rustic Woods High?"

She nodded again.

"This little reunion is very touching," said Abigail, "but I'd like to finish—"

"There's filing involved, right Ab?" Tate asked.

Flustered, Abigail answered. "Yes…"

"Can you file?" Tate asked Bunny.

"I'm very organized. Very. You'll see there on the application—I helped out for years in the front office of Tulip Tree Elementary when my kids were there. You can call Mrs. Sanchez. She'll vouch for me."

Tate caught Olga and Rupert exchanging glances, displeased that he'd decided to take over. They'd both opened their mouths several times, but never managed to get a word out. They were practically popping at the seams hoping to get their two cents in somewhere.

"Organized," Tate repeated. "Great. We need organized. And friendly, too? You can greet walk-ins and guests with a warm smile?"

"That's what I do best." Tate could see Bunny relaxing even though her stomach was still singing a chorus of its own.

Tate looked at his watch. "Twelve thirty. I've got a meeting with town planners at one, and I haven't eaten yet. Rupert, I know you're part of that meeting. Pretty sure Abigail and Olga have to be there too, right?"

They all nodded agreement. Rupert grumbled under his massive mustache. George mumbled something inaudible and surely unimportant.

"Thees meeting, it is mandatory!" huffed Olga, snapping her notebook shut.

Abigail shot Tate an evil eye, but did what he'd hoped she would. "Yes, well," said Crabby Abby. "I suppose we do need to end this interview then, Ms...Brogan?"

"Bergen," corrected Bunny.

"Right. Well, if we select you, we'll call and follow-up with an email. If not, well, I never enjoy being the bearer of bad news..."

Huh. She revels in bearing bad news, thought Tate.

"So if you don't hear from us," Abigail finished, "it means we hired someone more suited for the position. Thank you for coming."

Tate was the first to stand. He approached Bunny and offered his hand. "So you've stayed in Rustic Woods all these years?"

Bunny accepted his handshake. Her hands were very wet. "Sort of," she said as he noticed her green eyes and vaguely recalled another time he'd looked into them. He shook off the memory. Bleached blondes—not his type. Not that any woman had been "his type" for a while.

"Well, glad to see you again. Good luck with the job hunt." He waited until he'd left the conference room to wipe her sweat from his palms onto his jeans. He did hope she got the job though, and later, when he had a few minutes, he'd sweet talk Abigail, even though he knew she had no intention of hiring someone with hardly any work experience. Or anyone who looked like Bunny. Or who had the name, Bunny.

But for now, he needed to grab something to eat while tending to one of those emails he'd opened just before the interview started.

Three blocks from the Nature Center, in a small shopping plaza, was Garcia's Deli. Lonzo Garcia served an array of ethic foods that included pizza, burritos, nachos, sandwiches, bagels, salads, hamburgers, and gyros. And just because the food was delivered in record time didn't mean it lacked quality. Today, Tate was craving Mexican.

"Hey, Lonzo," he tipped his chin to the aproned man behind the counter. "Can I get a burrito today? Chicken and black beans."

"Sure, man. Salsa?"

"Make it mild."

"Mild?" Lonzo made a face as he spooned black beans onto the chicken covered tortilla. "You're wimping out today. Gettin' too old for the macho blend, eh?"

Tate raised an eyebrow while pulling his cell phone from his pocket. "Think so, my friend. Think so. And I'll take a bottle of water too, please."

Lonzo wrapped the burrito while a young woman rang up Tate's order. Tate scrolled through the contacts list on his phone, stopping to throw a ten dollar bill on the counter and grab his lunch. "Put the change in the tip jar," he said. Tate knew the woman, Inez, worked at Lonzo's six days a week, often more than eight hours a day, all for minimum wage. She had three kids at home—one who attended high school with his daughter, Willow. Lonzo had once confided that Inez saved every penny so she could put her son through college. Sometimes, when she wasn't looking, Tate would throw a twenty dollar bill into the tip jar.

Burrito and water in one hand, Tate pressed *dial* with his other, and walked to a bench at the end of the plaza. He waited for Colt Baron to pick up at the other end.

"Baron and Marr, Investigations."

"Colt?"

"Uh, no. Hang on a minute."

Tate heard the voice fade into the background. A moment later, his buddy was talking. "Yeah. This is Colt."

"Hey, it's Tate. You said to call. That your new partner?"

"Kilbourn! Dude. Good to hear from you. It's been a while. Yeah, that's Howard Marr. Howie for short. Howdie Doody when I want to crawl under his skin." There was some muffled talk and Colt laughed. "He's cool. So, about your brother."

"Right. So you do this kind of work?" Tate unwrapped the burrito with one hand and took a bite.

"Sure. No problemo. We need as much information as you can give us. Where he attended school, last known address, social security number, legal name as shown on his birth certificate. Quite honestly, not that hard."

"I was hoping a simple Google search would do the trick." Tate tried to talk around the burrito in his mouth. He swallowed. "Sorry, man. Eating on the run. Got a meeting in a few minutes."

"That's okay. Understand. If he's trying not to be found, internet searches won't help. You said he took off how long ago?"

"Thirty-four years."

"Holy crap. How old were you?"

Tate swallowed more burrito. He was eating too fast. The burrito wasn't going to sit well. "Six."

"Man. And he never got in touch again? With anyone in your family?"

"Not that I know of."

"Okay. Too bad. Well, send that info along with anything else you can think of, including hobbies, local friends from the area—anything, no matter how insignificant it seems."

Tate sipped from the water bottle. "I hate to ask, but how much will this cost me?"

"Don't worry about that. We're training Howard's wife, Barb, on these sorts of searches. If it's fairly easy, we won't charge a thing. If it looks like it's going to be more involved, we'll check with you first. How's that sound?"

"Generous. Can't thank you enough."

"Yeah, yeah. I get that all the time. Usually from a gorgeous and naked woman."

Tate heard a guffaw in the background and joined in the laughter. Colt's cocky jocularity was always good for a chuckle. He was the kind of guy who put on a good show to conceal a big heart. They'd met when Colt showed up one Saturday at the center as a volunteer for a stream clean-up. Generally the only people who showed up for those were the able elderly with a lot of time on their hands or kids needing to rack up volunteer requirements for school.

He had some crazy stories, Colt did. Especially surrounding his friend Barb. Tate had never met her, but she sounded like a handful. She'd even made the news a couple of times. That Howard must be a patient guy. But lucky at the same time, he guessed. At least his wife was still around.

Tate wolfed down the rest of the burrito, chased it with the water, threw the wrapper in the trash, bottle to recycling, and headed to the main offices of the Rustic Woods Association.

Planning meetings. His eyes rolled at the thought. He'd rather be taking advantage of the warmer-than-usual February day; canoeing the lakes and monitoring their shores.

Still, he didn't dare skip the meeting altogether. Bi-weekly planning meetings by the board were an annoyance worth dealing with because, generally, his position as lead naturalist in Rustic Woods was a dream job. Decent pay, he ran the show, and wasn't bothered much as long as he stayed out of other people's way. And, thanks to the donation by a wealthy family with a love for nature, he had the privilege of living in The Rustic House—a three bedroom modern ranch-style home on one of Rustic Woods' three lakes designed for environmental friendliness. As long as he maintained the house and property, he lived there rent-free, and his daughter could attend Rustic Woods High School which had one of the best reputations in the Northern Virginia/Washington, D.C. area.

So Tate fought the urge to snooze, made his opinion heard on two important topics regarding the paved nature trails, and, when the meeting was adjourned, waited at the door to talk to Abigail.

"Ab," he said, falling into step with her. "I wanted to—"

She held up a flat hand, cutting him off. "Nope. Nope, nope, nope." She shook her head vehemently.

"You don't even know what I'm going to say."

"You want me to hire that bimbo Brogan woman. You were drooling all over the table when she walked in."

"I was not drooling. And I think it was Bergen, not Brogan. She just—"

"What, were you high school sweethearts? Or did you have a crush on her? And now you see a way into her heart again and all that crap."

Only one woman had ever held Tate's heart, but he wasn't going to stoop to Crabby Abby's level and go there. She was a bitter woman who didn't deserve to ever know what was in his heart or his mind or his soul. "You're a fruitcake," he said, wishing he could flip her off at the same time. "I think she'd be good at the desk. People would like her."

"Calling me a fruitcake will go miles toward winning me to your side." She stopped abruptly and turned to give Tate a frigid glare. "The answer is no. I've made up my mind, and I'll make my offer tomorrow morning."

"If you don't intend to listen to my opinion, why was I there at all?"

"That was George's idea, not mine."

Yeah. George. Full of good ideas. Tate shrugged as Abigail stomped away. Well, he had tried his best.

His phone vibrated in his hip holster. A text from his dad. *Need hlp. When u come?* Tate felt his shoulders tighten. He'd have to go. He'd arranged to meet Willow at the Center after school got out. She was going to help him clear leaves away from the turtle pond, but that would have to wait now. And she should come with him, anyway. He decided to meet her as planned, and then they would check on Morton together.

CHAPTER THREE

BUNNY WAS DESPERATE FOR THAT glass of wine. She'd arrived at Barb's house, still shaking and stomach complaining like a cranky old man.

"Have you eaten today?" Barb asked Bunny.

Hmm. Bunny had to think about that. Yes. That's right—she'd had a poached egg before rushing off to be guillotined by Dr. Page. "Not much," she admitted. "But that noise you hear isn't hunger. It's raw nerves. My insides flip out when I'm upset."

"I'm putting food out anyway. You can't have wine on an empty stomach. We don't need you drunk before dinner, right?"

Her friend cut some pita wedges while Bunny sat at the kitchen table. "Maybe I should have a glass of water first." She noticed a severe dryness at the back of her throat when she swallowed.

"Coming up." Barb stopped chopping and filled a glass from her refrigerator, setting it in front of Bunny. "How did it go?" she asked, getting back to the pita.

Bunny chugged. The interview had been bad enough. Seeing Tate Kilbourn after all these years was even worse. She clunked the drained glass on the table. "It was awful.

There was this rude girl, and this creepy man, and a lady with this wild, frizzy hair who didn't smile..." Her hands flitted around her head describing Abigail's halo of frizz.

"Her hair didn't smile? How dare it?" Barb teased.

"You know what I mean."

"Yeah, but I got you to smile." Barb set a plate of pita and hummus on the table and poured Bunny a glass of white wine.

Bunny leaned back in her chair, pulling the glass with her. "The frizzy haired lady wasn't the worst part."

Barb narrowed her eyes. "Eat before drink, lady. Eat before drink."

Laughing, Bunny snatched a pita wedge, then scooped up a healthy serving of hummus. "Mm, that's good hummus," she said, covering her mouth politely as she talked while she chewed. "Really good." She washed it down with a sip of wine.

"What was the worst part?"

"It's going to sound so silly."

"Try me."

"Tate Kilbourn was there."

Barb exaggerated a shocked face. "You're right. That's so silly."

Bunny leaned against the table. "You don't understand. I've never stopped thinking about Tate. He was my high school crush. Through all of my boyfriends, and even my marriage, I never stopped dreaming about Tate."

"Even when you were with Russ, the super hot fireman? That's hard to believe."

"Even through Russ." Bunny sighed and sipped. "Don't ask me why. I haven't seen him since he graduated."

"Graduated high school or college?"

"High school."

"Man, Bunny. That's a long time to moon over someone."

She nodded and counted on her fingers. "Twenty-three years."

"How long did you date?"

"Oh, we didn't date. I told you—it was a crush. He was a senior, I was a sophomore. But he was so cute and *so* nice."

"So you knew each other? Had friends in common?"

Bunny shook her head. "I told you it was silly." It was silly. So, so silly. She gulped wine and set down the empty glass. "I'm not getting the job. I can feel it." She raked her hands through her hair, feeling the dried, split ends. "And I can't afford to keep coloring my hair. Maybe I should just chop it all off."

"That's a lot of chopping. You'd be bald. I have a better idea. Follow me."

Bunny was pleasantly surprised with her new look. At home, in her bathroom mirror, she admired the light chestnut brown which was much closer to her natural color. Barb had had several bottles of the wash-in rinse on hand. And she'd even given her a halfway decent trim to get rid of the split ends. *Not so bad*, she thought. *Not so bad*. Of course, she'd go through a dozen or more bottles of rinse before her own color grew out. Maybe she'd splurge on one last trip to the salon for a change back to her natural brown and be done with it.

But blond or brunette, Bunny had to face some facts. She wasn't going to get that job. The only person who'd asked any questions was Tate Kilbourn, and even he'd seemed bored when he asked them. And that Abigail lady was just plain scary. Bunny wasn't sure she'd want to work for her.

As much as she hated the idea, she might have to ask Daddy for help. She had a couple of months to find a job, but everyone said the job market was lean. Even high school and college kids had trouble finding work. Her son Charlie had been putting in applications all around town and no one was calling back. And he was a good kid with good grades. Responsible. The kind of kid they'd want to hire.

Bunny sighed and picked up the phone. She let it ring twenty times before hanging up. Daddy hated answering machines and phone service voicemail—he couldn't figure out how to operate them. Consequently, when she couldn't reach him in his apartment at the Whispering Pines Retirement Community, she had to leave a message at their front desk. Luckily, Nice Nancy answered. She was always kind and helpful toward Bunny.

"Nancy, this is Bunny Bergen. I'm trying to reach Daddy. Are you able to see if he's in the community room before I leave a message?"

"Oh." Right away, Nice Nancy sounded apprehensive. "Hi, Ms. Bergen. Um..."

"Is there a problem?"

"Well..." Bunny could hear Nancy pull the phone from her mouth and speak to someone else, but the words were too muted to understand. A moment later, another voice spoke in Bunny's ear.

"Ms. Burkett, this is Dan Baker, the day manager. I'm afraid we are not authorized to discuss your father or his condition at this time."

"His condition? Is something wrong?"

"Again, we are not authorized to disclose any information regarding Douglas Hobbs. You would need to direct any inquiries to the person who holds his power of attorney."

"Power of attorney? Just tell me if he's alive, for crying out loud!"

"I will need to end this call now, Ms. Burkett."

"It's Bergen you...you..." she slammed the phone down, shaking. "Demon!" she screamed, knowing the person to blame for her black-listing. She took a minute to calm herself, not wanting a shaky voice when she got on the phone with her demon sister. She was so upset, though. What had happened to Daddy? If something was wrong, why hadn't anyone called her?

After several minutes, Bunny realized she was only talking herself into more worry, so with trembling hands, she picked the phone back up and dialed her sister, who picked up almost immediately.

"Bun Bun," she said in her usual, patronizing tone, "why are you causing problems with the staff at the Pines? I just got off the phone with Dan who was very troubled after you threatened him."

"I didn't threaten him, Deena! Where's Daddy?"

"I can tell you're upset—"

"Would you answer my question?"

Her sister, who always had to control conversations, purposely waited several seconds before proceeding. "He's in the hospital."

"Is he okay? What's wrong? How long?"

"Which one of those questions do you want me to answer first?"

"Oh my God!" Bunny shouted into the phone.

"Settle down. You're so full of drama. He's fine. A little weak still, but fine."

"Why weak? What *happened*, Deena?"

"He didn't want anyone to know. He was embarrassed. I'm only acting on his request."

Still no information. Bunny wasn't stupid. Deena-the-Demon had reveled in working the bossy older sister angle her entire life. Bunny wasn't going to stay on the phone playing her cat and mouse game anymore. "What hospital, Deena? Is it Rustic Woods? Because I'll march over there right now and cause a scene if you don't tell me everything you know."

"See, that's exactly why Daddy put me in charge. You still behave like a child when decorum is in order. He slipped and fell in his bathroom. They kept him for observation. He'll probably be released tomorrow morning, and you can visit him at the Pines once he gives me the okay. I told you, he's very embarrassed. Don't make this out to be more than it is."

"Promise you'll call me tomorrow and let me know what's happening?"

"Promise, little Bun Bun. I have to go now. Things to do." Her sister made smooching noises in Bunny's ear. Bunny responded by sticking her finger in her mouth, pretending to make herself gag, then slammed the cordless house phone back into its charging cradle.

One day, Demon, she thought. *One day*. As a child, Bunny had spent hours dreaming of cruel and unusual ways to get back at her sister over the years, and *One day, Demon*, had become her classic mantra. She'd never had the courage or stamina to actually fight her. But one day...

She heard her cell phone buzz across the room. It was a text from her son Charlie. He was staying after school to retake a test. Her younger son, Michael, was staying after as well, taking the late bus home. Neither of them knew she'd been fired—they'd figure she was still at work. What should she do with her unexpected day off, home alone? She needed something to take her mind off Daddy and Demon.

She flipped through some papers on her dining room table. Bills. She didn't want to open them. And there was a flier with a note stickied to it. *Mom, can you order my yearbook? Charlie.* She looked more closely at the flier. Eighty-five dollars for a yearbook. They'd gone up. She remembered when her own cost twenty dollars, and that had included her name embossed on the cover, for crying out loud.

Hmm...her yearbook. Now there was a way to take her mind off her worries. Pictures of Tate Kilbourn.

CHAPTER FOUR

TATE HELD THE PAPER IN one hand, staring at it, while he thumbed his cell phone with the other. In less than a week, Colt had located his brother, Samuel. Now, against his sister's wishes, he had an address and a phone number for the man none of them had seen in more than three decades. And for what?

Tate wondered if he was being honest with himself. If Samuel really cared at all, or had an ounce of interest in them, he would have returned at some point, right? Or sought them out. Was he doing this for his father, or was he justifying his own need to know the older brother he'd only created in his imagination from pictures and the words of his sister?

The phone rang in his hand. Damn. It was May. She had an eerie ability to read his mind. Like a mother. Only she wasn't his mother, she was his sister. She'd only been forced to play the part of his mother.

Tate hesitated. He hadn't told May that he'd decided to find Samuel, only that he once had the idea. Her reaction hadn't exactly been supportive. He let the phone ring again, and again, not sure if he wanted to answer. Ah, hell. "Yeah, May, what's up?"

"Caught you on a good day, did I?"

"Just busy. I'm at work. Is this urgent?"

"How's Morton?"

"He has his good days and his bad. You didn't come the other day—you said you would."

"Right. Sorry. Things got bloody awful around here and I just couldn't, blah, blah, blah."

May had two nasty habits in Tate's mind: she loved the word bloody, and she ended sentences with *blah, blah, blah*. She didn't end all sentences that way, but enough to make him want to yank her tongue out when she did. She was also the architect of her own life disasters, of which there seemed to be many. But he attributed that to the artist in her and largely forgave her because she'd more or less been the only mother he'd known.

"Probably best," he said. "It was one of his bad days. Is that why you called?"

"No, you ornery oaf. Did she hear about the part yet? Was she cast?"

That made him smile. May did love her niece. "Not yet. She said they'll announce today. In fact," he looked at the clock on the wall of his small office, "I'd better get home. I want to be there when she got off the bus."

Tate's daughter, Willow, had set her hopes high when she auditioned for the spring musical at Rustic Woods High. Since she was a sophomore and new to the school, Tate feared her dreams of snagging the lead role in *Kiss Me, Kate* were a bit lofty. May, a gifted singer and dancer herself, had helped Willow practice, and, in Tate's mind, contributed to the unrealistic goal.

He hoped Willow would be happy with a smaller role, or the chorus, although, truthfully, he did believe she deserved more. He just felt it was important to keep your head closer to the ground. He knew more than anybody that you didn't always get what you wanted in this world.

"Okay," sighed May. "She did say she'd text me, but I thought I'd check since I hadn't heard."

"I'll make sure she lets you know." For a split second, he thought he'd mention that he had Samuel's contact information in his hand; then thought better of it. He hadn't decided what to do with it. "Don't be a stranger. Mort will want to see you."

"Don't bloody kid yourself. Or me."

"Whatever you say, May. Talk to you soon."

"Hey, Tater Tot..."

"Yeah?"

"Love you."

"Love you, too."

Tate ended the call, slipped the paper with Samuel's number into his back pocket, lifted his coat from the back of his chair and ran out the door, passing the empty reception desk on his way.

Crabby Abby still hadn't hired anyone. Apparently, her first choice had a better offer. Imagine that. A man with two degrees got a better offer than becoming a receptionist for a small nature center.

Tate shook his head. He had to give Abby a little credit for not asking the rude temp-hire back, at least. Having her answer the phones was worse than no one answering them.

He caught George's eye on the way out. "Done for the day, man. Have a good weekend." George gave him a queer look, which Tate was used to, since queer looks were about all the pointy nosed man seemed capable of.

Once home, Tate, figuring he had a few minutes before hearing a yay or nay from Willow via text, phoned his father's house.

"Hello?" answered the nurse.

"Hi, Clara. It's Tate. How is he today?"

"Good. He's napping now, though."

"That's okay. Don't wake him."

"He's asking for the sweet yogurt," she said. "I don't know what that is. He won't eat what's there."

Tate rolled his eyes. The man was like a two-year-old sometimes. "Sweet yogurt is vanilla. He stopped eating it ages ago and said he only wanted blueberry."

"Well, now he wants sweet."

Mort probably needed more than yogurt, so a grocery store run was in order anyway to stock his father's fridge. "Tell him he'll have sweet as soon as I can get it."

"Sounds good. Should I tell him when you'll stop by?"

"Tomorrow."

"Okay. And, um...Mr. Kilbourn, my manager told me to tell you that unless your insurance pays on the latest claim, you'll either need to pay the balance owed, or I can't come next week. I'm sorry, I hate to have to talk money. Not why I became a nurse."

"I understand. Don't worry. The insurance company is playing games again. I'll send a check from Mort...from my father's account to pay the balance." He always felt strange calling his father by his first name to people other than family. He and May, as long as he could remember, had always called him Morton instead of Dad. It was a respect issue, he figured. The man didn't really command enough to warrant the title. "I'll call your manager and let her know money is on the way."

"That's okay, I'll be talking to her when I leave here. I'll tell her."

"Thanks, Clara."

Tate pulled the paper from his back pocket and stared at his own scribbling. Why did he feel so compelled to call this...this stranger, really, and tell him that their father was dying? Morton didn't want it. At least, that's what he claimed anytime Tate brought up the subject. He had an address—maybe Tate should just write a letter. It would be easier. If it needed to be done at all.

He heard the front door open. Willow? She hadn't texted him with any news. His heart sank for her. It couldn't be good. "Sweetie, is that you?"

"Yeah." Her voice was low. Her backpack thumped against the floor. Tate imagined her at the front door, shoulders slumped, possibly with tears in her eyes. She didn't even get a part in the chorus? He shoved the paper in his pocket and rounded the corner from the living room to their small foyer, ready to give her a sympathetic hug.

Only her shoulders weren't slumped, and her eyes weren't filled with tears. His beautiful daughter with her wavy blond hair had a sly grin on her fair, freckled face and a twinkle in her deep brown eyes.

"You got the part?" he asked.

She nodded, her grin widening to a broad, happy smile. "Yup! Yup! I did it!" She jumped in his arms, and he swung her around, hugging her tightly. "I did it, Daddy!"

"The lead?" he asked setting her back down.

She shook her head. "Better—Lois Lane! Who, by the way, is not Superman's girlfriend. I kind of play two roles because Lois is in a musical version of *The Taming of the Shrew*—that's Shakespeare—so I'm playing Lois, who plays Bianca. A play within a play. Did I tell you that already? Anyway, it's almost the lead, and I like her role better. We start rehearsals Monday."

She bugged her eyes out at him. "Monday! Can you believe it?" She lifted the backpack from the floor and hefted it back onto her shoulder, giving Tate's arm a loving rub. "There's a Facebook page set up already. I'm going to go check it out."

"Tell you what, let's celebrate. I'll take you out to dinner."

"Fiorenza's?"

"It's a date."

Tate watched his daughter walk down the hall to her room, a definite skip in her step. She walked just like her mother. "Hey, did you text Aunt May?"

She turned. "Yeah. She's psyched."

In the kitchen, Tate poured himself a glass of water and practically chugged it. A trick he'd learned for pushing emotion away when it threatened to overtake him. When the danger of losing control had passed, he texted May. *Join us for dinr if u can. Fiorenza's. 6pm.*

CHAPTER FIVE

I T HAD BEEN SEVERAL DAYS since Bunny's firing and subsequent disastrous job interview. The Nature Center had not called, and since that Abigail woman had told her no news was bad news, Bunny was feeling lower than low.

And Demon had broken her promise. She had never called to let Bunny know how Daddy was doing. Bunny had finally reached him on her own. He was back in his apartment, although his voice sounded weak. He said he'd love to see her, so Bunny prettied up for a visit.

Some days, she liked to take him out for a walk and fresh air. He especially liked the Larkspur Gardens, but the weather had turned cold, and such a trek would be out of the question. She decided instead to fix him a pot of chicken and dumplings and take it over along with a DVD. They always enjoyed watching movies together.

When she hit the lobby at Whispering Pines, hands burdened by the pot of chicken, Bunny found it difficult to push the button for the elevator. From the main desk, Nice Nancy saw her struggling and ran over to help out. "Hi, Mrs. Bergen," Nice Nancy said, pressing her thumb to the button. "How are you today?"

"Fine, Nancy, thanks. And it's Ms. now. Not married anymore."

Nice Nancy nodded. "That's right. I keep forgetting. Hey," she paused and Bunny feared an admonishment was coming for some new transgression. "I'm so sorry about the other day, Ms. Bergen. You shouldn't have been treated so badly."

Bunny shook her head. At the same time, the elevator bell chimed, alerting her that the doors would open momentarily. She shifted the pot a bit. "Don't worry, Nancy. I know you're just following orders."

Nice Nancy nodded again, more vigorously this time, and lowered her voice to a whisper. "She puts her nose into everything around here." The doors began to open. "But you didn't hear that from me." With that, Nice Nancy gave a quick squeeze to Bunny's arm and scooted back to her station. Bunny stepped into the elevator after allowing the elderly couple inside to exit.

On her ascent to the fifth floor, Bunny shifted the uncomfortable pot again, and worried about Nice Nancy's comment. *What the heck was Demon up to?*

Finally, with aching arms, Bunny arrived in front of Daddy's apartment. She managed to balance the pot briefly with one hand in order to punch the doorbell with the other. When he didn't arrive in a reasonable time, she tried the knob.

It was locked. Afraid the chicken and dumplings would spill if she attempted another balancing act, she placed the pot on the floor and knocked loudly.

Nothing.

She knocked louder. "Daddy!" *Knock, knock, knock.* "Daddy!" Her pitch rose several octaves. A door behind her opened.

"I just texted him, honey. It takes him a minute to get to the doah."

Bunny didn't need to turn around to know the voice was Yetta Lipman, a widow who had dated Daddy once. The date hadn't gone so well, but they had learned to be friends.

"You texted him?" Bunny asked, noting that Yetta must have just woken from a mid-morning nap. Her shocking orange hair was oddly flat on one side. "He doesn't have a cell phone. He hates them."

Yetta shook her head. "Deena got 'im one."

"And he can use it?"

Yetta shrugged. "Some days yes, some days, no." Then she frowned. "But he can annihilate aliens with the best of 'em."

Daddy's door flew open, startling Bunny, who was still in shock that her father owned a device he once condemned as the future downfall of America. As for the alien comment, the woman must have still been groggy from her nap.

"Today must be a yes day," Yetta coughed, then closed her door.

Bunny picked up her pot, a little frazzled. "You had me worried, Daddy."

"Why are you here?" grumbled Douglas Hobbs. "I'm not up for visitors right now." His face was drawn and white, and he stood hunched far more than usual. He rested the weight of his thin frame on a cane. He'd been nearly bald for several years, but she noticed that he had shaved his head entirely now.

"Daddy," she said, "we talked on the phone this morning. You said to come over. I brought you chicken and dumplings." She held up the pot to show him.

He shook his head. "Can't after all. I got plans."

"Plans? You didn't mention any—"

Douglas Hobbs threw his arm in the air and nearly toppled himself in the process. His face pinched in anger. "I got plans! Don't you listen to anything I say?"

"You're right, Daddy. I'm sorry. Can I at least bring this in for you?"

"What is it?"

"Chicken and dumplings."

"Fine, fine. Do what you want." He shuffled backwards, allowing Bunny enough room to squeeze past. The apartment was small, just a tiny entrance with a small kitchen right off, a two-person dining area, a living room a mouse might find comfortable, a bedroom and handicapped bathroom. Daddy wasn't handicapped, but all of the bathrooms at Whispering Pines were handicap-ready. This annoyed him, and he let Bunny know repeatedly *how much* it annoyed him.

It annoyed her how much it annoyed him. She placed the pot on the counter in the dimly lit Cracker Jack box of a kitchen. She reached to the cupboard to find two bowls.

"Jeez-a-Louey, girl. What are you doing now?"

"Getting bowls for our lunch."

"Lunch? I'm taking a nap. Put it in the fridge and make sure the door is locked on your way out." He pointed an arthritic finger at the door as he shuffled toward the bedroom. "Nobody around here listens to anything I say. A person deserves to be treated better."

Bunny closed the cupboard door and watched him retreat. He had "plans," but he was going to take a nap. He'd had his grumpy moments before, but this was the worst she'd ever seen.

She placed the pot in the refrigerator as instructed, then took a moment to look around before leaving. The curtains to the only window—a sliding glass door that opened onto a balcony—were drawn. The television was off.

She picked up a bowl that was half-full of hours-old oatmeal. The infamous cell phone rested on the side table near the loveseat.

Bunny tiptoed over, bowl still in her hands, and lifted the phone for a look-see. It was an old Blackberry with a keypad, which was probably easier for him to use than a smartphone. Yetta's text was still on the display: *open your door dh!*

Bunny smiled at Yetta's nickname—one day she started calling him DH and never quit. Daddy pretended he hated it, but Bunny thought he secretly enjoyed the personal touch.

She punched and scrolled through menus until she found the phone's number, but with a bowl in one hand and the phone in the other, she was forced to commit it to memory. She'd write it down as soon as she got out of the apartment.

Placing the phone back on the side table as quietly as possible, she took another scan of the apartment for other dirty dishes, then tiptoed back to the kitchen where she emptied the bowl of crusty oatmeal. She left the bowl in the sink to soak. Let Demon come and clean it, she thought.

On her way out, she checked the doorknob to make sure it was locked.

When the elevators opened on the first floor, Bunny spotted Nice Nancy still at the desk. She was alone. Good. Maybe if Bunny sweet talked her, she'd give up a little information.

She readjusted the purse on her shoulder, smiled , and walked to the front desk as if she just wanted to stop and say hello.

Nice Nancy returned the smile. "Did you have a nice visit?" she asked Bunny.

"It's always nice to see Daddy," Bunny said, leaning on the tall desk in front of her. "He and I were talking about how much he enjoys it here. Especially you and the other staff. You really do make things very comfortable for the seniors here, Nancy. I'm not sure I show my appreciation nearly enough."

"I'm glad he's happy."

Bunny tilted her head and tapped a finger on the desk. "I'm worried, though." She waited to see if Nice Nancy would invite further discussion. The woman, however, let the smile drop from her face and began sorting the envelopes in her hands.

Bunny forged on. "He seemed agitated."

Nice Nancy snapped her eyes back up from the envelopes and locked onto Bunny's gaze. "I'll get fired, Ms. Bergen," she whispered. "I can't."

"You can't what?" asked a man, who rounded the corner from a hallway behind the desk. He gave Bunny a courteous but short tip of the head. "Ms. Bergen."

Bunny resisted the urge to curse under her breath at the sight of Dan Baker. "Mr. Baker," she responded.

"What can't you do, Nancy?" the man asked.

Bunny thought she might faint. Lying and deceit weren't her forte. She'd once worried for weeks over telling the school that Charlie was sick when she was really taking him and his brother to see the Cherry Blossoms near the Jefferson Memorial.

Nancy, however, barely blinked an eye before offering a piece of fiction worth publishing. "The Rustic Woods Winter Wine and Cheese Fest this weekend. Ms. Bergen was wondering if I was going, but I can't."

Wow, Bunny wanted to take lessons from Nice Nancy. She was good.

"You like wine?"

It took Bunny a minute to realize that Dan Baker was addressing her. "Me?" She pointed to herself. "Sure." She nodded. *Love it. Wish I had a glass right now. Or a bottle.* "Sure."

The air filled with awkward silence. Bunny tried to hide the fact that her hands were shaking, but then her cell phone rang in her purse.

She pulled it out, wanting to look nonchalant and in control, but nearly dropped the thing from trembling so badly. She managed to make out the number on the display. "I, uh...don't recognize this number," she apologized to Nice Nancy and Mr. Baker. "I'll take this outside." She gave a wave and scooted out as fast as she could, clicking answer once she was through the automatic doors. "Hello?"

The female voice on the other end sounded familiar, but Bunny couldn't immediately place it. "Is this Robin Bergen?"

That was odd. Bunny never used her real name...except on the application for the job at the Rustic Woods Nature Center. Could it be? "Yes." Bunny's voice went shaky. "This is Ms. Bergen."

"This is Abigail from the Nature Center. We would like to offer you the receptionist position. If you are still interested, that is."

Bunny celebrated by picking up a sandwich and chips from Garcia's Deli. Lonzo made the best roast beef and cheddar around, and it came with a dill pickle spear to die for. Lonzo's sister-in-law, Ria Sanchez, was the nicest little lady—she worked at Tulip Tree Elementary where both of her boys had gone. She had always been wonderfully kind to Bunny, whom she called, "Mees Boony."

At home, Bunny placed the sandwich, chips, and pickle on a nice plate and poured herself a half-glass of wine. She ate alone, but content, at her large dining room table.

She had another job. She'd do this one right. She'd dress the part and show everyone what a valuable asset she could be. The pay wasn't great—only fourteen dollars an hour. She'd never be able to keep her house with that kind of salary, but then again, she'd already resigned herself to putting it on the market.

She'd been thinking of asking Daddy for more money, but in the last few days, even before seeing him in his poor state today, she'd decided the time had come for her to take better control of her financial affairs. She couldn't rely on men her entire life.

She had her fingers crossed that there was enough equity in her house to make a hefty down payment on a smaller townhouse or maybe a condo. Once Charlie left for college, it would only be her and Michael. They could manage in a three bedroom condo if necessary.

She chewed some more, kind of excited to be thinking of making big changes in her life. And she'd be working with Tate Kilbourn. Her life problems caused her an awful lot of worry, but the thought of working with Tate was worrisome and exhilarating all at the same time.

As Bunny cleared crumbs from her plate into the kitchen sink, the front door opened. She looked at the clock, surprised by the time. "Charlie?" she called out.

"Yeah." Charlie wasn't big on words, but most moms of teen boys told her that was par for the course. His footsteps moved toward the stairs rather than the kitchen.

"Charlie, come here. I have good news."

The footsteps changed direction, and in due time, her son was leaning in the kitchen doorway, his backpack slung over one shoulder. He was a really good looking kid; slim but muscular build, dark hair, green eyes. "I have good news, too," he said with a slight smile.

"Really? What's yours? You go first." She had no idea what his good news could be. He'd taken the SATs, but she knew those scores wouldn't be released for another week.

"I got a part in the school musical."

"Did you audition?"

"Yeah, Mom, I auditioned."

"You didn't tell me about it."

He shrugged. "It was kind of last minute. You know, just to see."

"That's very exciting, then!" She clapped her hands. "What's the play? What part?"

"*Kiss Me, Kate*. I'm playing Bill Calhoun. I'll be honest, I don't know anything about the play. Have you seen it?"

She shook her head. "Sorry. Can't help you there. Guess you'll have to read it. Since, you know, you're in it and all." She gave him a hug. "I'm so proud of you!"

Charlie shrugged again. "We'll see. What's your good news?"

"Your mother has another job. I start Monday."

His smile was genuine. "Cool. Where?"

"The Nature Center."

He gave her a sideways look. "Nature Center? You're hardly a nature girl."

"Receptionist, silly. I'll be answering phones, not... catching beavers. Or whatever they do. Anyway, it's a job. I'm excited."

He nodded. "So am I. About your job I mean."

"Shall I make you a snack?"

"Nah." He turned to leave. "There's a Facebook page set up for the cast. I'm going to go check it out."

"Hey, Charlie," Bunny called to stop him, "who's in charge of the play?"

"In charge? What do you mean?"

"The director, I guess? Who's running the show at the school?"

He shrugged again. Always with the shrugging, this boy. "The theater teacher, I guess."

"What's her name?"

"I don't know."

"You don't know her name?"

"Can't remember. It's not like I'm a theater geek or something, you know."

"Okay..."

He started up the stairs. "Hey, Charlie," she said again.

"What, Mom?"

"Let's celebrate tonight after Michael's soccer practice. Dinner at Fiorenza's."

Charlie smiled. Thank goodness he didn't shrug again. "Yeah. That'd be great."

CHAPTER SIX

ATE NEVER HEARD BACK FROM May. He didn't know if she'd make it for dinner, but he and Willow got a table for three anyway. You never quite knew what May was going to do, so it was better to be prepared.

Tate ordered a draft beer, and Willow asked for a soda. Seated at a square table near the rear of the long and narrow family restaurant, they looked over the menu while waiting for their drinks to arrive.

"I don't know why you even pretend to look," Willow teased as they both scanned the large, laminated menus in their hands. "You know you'll get the lasagna."

One corner of his mouth lifted as he eyed her in playful reprimand. "You never know. I just might surprise you."

"Do it," she said, her smile widening. She lowered the menu and leaned over the table. "I dare you."

"See, now I love a dare."

"Be wild."

"In case you haven't noticed, wild is what I do for a living."

"I'm talking about moving outside of your comfort zone, old man."

About to make some sort of fun retort to the attack on his age, Tate stopped when he saw May breezing their way. Breezy and flowy—that's how Tate described May. As if she floated on the wind. Her dark wavy hair, streaked liberally with silver highlights, fell below her shoulders and never seemed quite tamed, yet always looked stunning. She was twelve years his senior, yet, despite the many gray strands, barely looked five years older than Tate. Today she was dressed in a typical May ensemble—long, vibrant peasant skirt, silky blouse, a deep purple sweater that seemed to cascade from her shoulders like a waterfall, dangly earrings with every color of the spectrum represented.

Tate smiled, glad she'd come. They were very different, but she meant an awful lot to him and to Willow. She'd helped him through the very roughest years; years when he wasn't sure he'd make another day. He waved a hand to catch her attention, but she'd already seen them.

"My daughter just called me an old man," Tate said when she was almost to the table. He stood and pulled a chair our for his sister.

May's blue eyes twinkled. She kissed Willow on the cheek and squeezed her shoulder before sitting in the offered chair. "She can do or say anything she wants. She's a star now, and stars can say whatever they bloody want to."

Tate sat back down and May grabbed his hand for a loving squeeze. "This is about the lasagna, isn't it?" She looked at Willow. "Did he order the lasagna again?"

Willow giggled. "He says he'll surprise me."

Tate shrugged. "I believe my exact words were, 'I might surprise you.'"

"Well," said May, picking up the menu in front of her, "you know what they say..."

Their waitress appeared with the beer and soda on a tray, so Tate didn't bother to figure out if May intended to eventually finish that thought.

The young woman placed the drinks on the table and retrieved a pad and pen from her apron. "Would you like to hear our specials?" she asked.

"We'd *especially* love to hear the specials!" May exclaimed.

May always added drama to a dinner table, Tate thought, smiling inwardly.

Momentarily startled by May's abundant energy, the waitress cleared her throat and gave her spiel. "Our soup of the day is Pastini in Brodo—that's tiny pasta in chicken broth. We have Pesce Spada, which is a grilled swordfish filet seasoned with rosemary and thyme and served with mushroom risotto. And the chef's special, which is Veal Limone—veal medallions sautéed with white wine and onions, and topped with a lemon sauce. That's served with asparagus spears."

The girl readied herself with pen to pad. She looked at Willow. "Ma'am, what would you like?"

Willow tipped her head back and forth a couple of times, thinking her options over, then snapped the menu shut. "I'll have the soup of the day and the large Mediterranean salad."

"Ooo. That sounds good," said May. "I'll have that too. No onions though. Does that come with onions?" She waved her hand around. "Definitely no onions."

The waitress scribbled and repeated, "No onions."

"And the dressing on the side please," added May. Then she pointed to Tate. "And he'll have that swordfish dish because he's neither old nor boring." She and Willow laughed in unison.

Tate frowned. "I never said anything about being boring."

"Will there be anything else?" asked the waitress.

"No, that's all," he said. Tate noticed the girl didn't wear a name tag. "And your name is?"

"I'm sorry," she said. "My name is Angela. I'll be your server. I was supposed to open with that line."

Tate liked knowing the names of waiters and waitresses he dealt with. He'd been a waiter in college, and while there had been many good customers, the bad ones stuck out in his mind. He liked to address waitstaff by name and tip well for good service rendered. "Thank you, Angela." He handed her his menu. "That swordfish—is it good?"

"I'm not a fish person myself, so I haven't tasted it, but the people at that table over there," she indicated a couple just getting up to leave, "said it was exceptional. They were really happy with it."

May patted Tate's hand as the waitress left to tend another table. "It's okay, little brother. You can try new things."

"I try plenty of new things," Tate said, still smiling. He held up his beer. "This beer is new."

"How exciting for you, blah, blah, blah," May said, grinning. She turned to Willow. "Speaking of exciting. Tell me about this Charlie. Is he very cute?"

Tate saw Willow's cheeks blush and wondered what he was missing. "Who's Charlie?" he asked, and then realized he was probably stepping into sensitive teenage girl territory. He wasn't always quick on the uptake about these things. Of course, May shouldn't have brought it up if it was sensitive.

"Charlie Bergen. He's the guy who was cast as Bill Calhoun. Sort of the love interest to my Lois."

"And he has an eye for our Willow."

"Aunt May!"

"It's okay," May said airily. "He can know these things." She turned to Tate. "She kinda thinks he's cute too…"

Willow buried her face in her hands. "Oh my God."

The name clicked in Tate's mind. Bergen. A picture of Bunny flashed in his mind, not of the beautiful but self-conscious woman in the interview, but of the lovely girl he'd hardly known in high school. A girl he'd danced with just once. "Bergen. Is his mother Bunny Bergen?"

Willow uncovered her crimson face. "I don't know. I barely know him."

"They're in the same photography class, but he's a junior, and they talk, and she thinks he might ask her to prom."

"Oh my God, Aunt May. I'm never going to tell you anything again."

Tate noticed that Willow was obviously embarrassed, but not all that horrified. He was glad May had outed her. These on-the-verge-of-womanhood moments were the times that worried him most about being a single father to a growing girl. He wanted to know what was happening in his daughter's life, and from the way she looked across the table, red-faced but smiling, he guessed that she wanted him to know as well.

He sipped from his glass and offered a warm smile. "The guy would be crazy not to ask you."

Willow avoided eye contact, playing with her fork. "Thanks," she said after a pause. Her cheeks reddened again. The smile stretched more broadly across her face. "I'll be seeing a lot of him now, so I guess if he's crazy, it will become apparent pretty fast."

Tate watched his daughter, proud of the beauty she carried on the inside, sad that her mother couldn't see it, too. Willow was so much like her.

When the food arrived, the three of them chatted about Willow's classes at school, about May's new art piece for a show in Alexandria, and about the unusually warm late-February weather.

Tate had Samuel and his phone number on his mind, but decided he should not bring it up. This was a celebration dinner, and he didn't want to ruin Willow's excitement by possibly upsetting May by bringing up the brother who had deserted them.

Tate paid the bill, adding more than twenty percent for Angela, the waitress, and the three of them rose to leave. "So, you'll stop by to see Morton soon, right?" he asked his sister.

"Absolutely, love." She put her arm around his. "I have things going on tomorrow, but I'll find time on Sunday. Tuesday at the latest."

Willow walked just in front of them toward the front of the restaurant.

"Kilbourn! Hey, man. How's it goin'?" Tate followed the sound of the voice, and spotted his buddy, Colt Baron, standing with a group of people at the hostess podium.

"Hey," Tate said smiling. "Good, thanks. You?"

"Tate, these are my friends Howard and Barb Marr." Colt looked at the woman with the curly hair. "Barb, this is Tate Kilbourn—the guy you did the research for."

Tate winced, feeling a disaster coming on and not knowing how to stop it.

Sure enough, Colt's friend Barb, the one he had heard the crazy stories about, opened her mouth. "Oh, the Kilbourn case. Right." She smiled at Tate, then her face brightened and eyes popped as if she'd had an epiphany. "Tate. You're Tate." She nodded while giving him a definite once over, as if he were a new car she might want to purchase. With her husband standing right there, too. Man, she was as bizarre as he'd heard.

"Nice to meet you, Tate," she said with a slow nod.

Well, at least she didn't mention Samuel in front of May. He was relieved about that at least. He just wished the Marr woman would stop staring at him. He could see Willow contemplating what Colt had said about research, her eyebrows doing that thing they do when she was getting ready to question him. Tate jumped into a conversation with Barb quickly before Willow could open her mouth and ask what Colt was talking about.

"Nice to meet you as well, Barb. I've heard a lot about you." He introduced Willow to Colt and his friends. "And this is my sister, May," he continued. When May giggled like a school girl, he realized she was giving Colt some very obvious doe eyes. He suppressed an eye roll.

Colt reached out to shake May's hand. "Hi May," he said. "Tate never mentioned he had a beautiful sister."

The door of the restaurant opened, triggering a bell. Tate watched two boys enter. One had dark hair and looked older than the smaller blonde boy. Almost immediately, the older boy's face lit with a wide smile, and Tate noticed he was looking at Willow.

A quick glance at Willow's red face made him wonder if this was the boy in the play, but the answer was following just on the boy's heels—Bunny Bergen. She looked different than she had at the interview. With a jolt, he realized it was her hair. It was brown now. Nice.

She was stunning. Clear, fair skin, statuesque. Eyes that seemed to tell a story. Eyes that locked briefly onto his, causing his gut to churn and his palms to sweat. She dropped her gaze as if embarrassed.

Tate was shaken by his reaction. He hadn't felt that kind of attraction to a woman in a long, long time.

The Marr woman broke his trance. "Bunny!"

Bunny locked eyes with Tate again before turning to Barb, who was waving her over.

CHAPTER SEVEN

UNNY THOUGHT ABOUT TATE KILBOURN all weekend long.

After seeing him Friday night at Fiorenza's, how could she not? They'd had a short exchange—he'd been surprised to find out she'd been hired by the Nature Center. Bunny couldn't tell if it was good surprised or bad surprised. That worried her, since she'd be seeing him daily from now on.

Then Barb had pulled her aside and whispered, "OMG, he's so hot!" Barb's husband, Howard looked like George Clooney, so Barb was someone with obviously high standards. And Barb was right. Tate was hot. Steamy hot. He'd grown a beard that he kept trimmed close to his strong jaw, and the slight peppering of silver hairs made it especially sexy, she thought. His brown eyes were so intensely dark that she felt like she was looking into a well with infinite depth. And he was tall. Taller than Bunny by three or four inches, which was especially sexy since she fell just an inch short of six feet herself. Tall men weren't easy to find.

Monday morning, Bunny was a mess. She'd tossed and turned most of the night, worrying about her first day on the new job. At five a.m. she decided to give up and got out of bed to start her day with a strong cup of coffee.

She got on the computer and looked up the theater teacher's name at Rustic Woods High School. The woman's name was Ms. Steffler.

Bunny sent her an email offering to help with the play in any way needed. She told Ms. Steffler in the short but sweet email that she always "supported the school in any way she could," and asked the teacher to please reply and let her know "what sorts of volunteer positions are needed for the production of *Kiss Me, Kate*. Sincerely, Bunny Bergen, Charlie's mom."

Truthfully, Bunny hadn't volunteered in her sons' middle and high schools the way she had when they were in elementary school, and she felt badly about that. She'd let her divorce and the child custody fight overwhelm her ability to give back to the community. Now was the perfect time to get involved again. It felt good to have something to be involved in.

Bunny showered, made lunches for her boys and got them out of the house in time for their buses. By the time she'd eaten a slice of toast and half cup of yogurt—more for energy since nerves had cut her appetite—and packed her own small lunch, it was still only seven a.m. She didn't need to be at the Nature Center until nine.

Oh well, maybe she could just take her time dressing, blow drying her hair, and putting on her makeup. She'd take it nice and slow.

She had asked Barb to assist her on a shopping trip over the weekend to select some Nature Center appropriate work attire. She'd come away with two turtlenecks—white and black—a teal fleece vest, two pairs of fancier-style jeans—black and khaki—a nice, but subdued flannel shirt in tones of brown that she could wear over either turtleneck, and, of all things, a pair of hiking boots.

The wardrobe was so vastly different from anything Bunny had ever worn that even Barb expressed concern about Bunny's choices. "You only want to dress a little more conservatively than you're used to, Bunny," she'd said. "Not transform into a poster girl for Forest Service recruitment. I mean, those boots. They're kind of chunky."

But Bunny had made up her mind. She wouldn't lose another job for dressing incorrectly. She'd do this one right. She'd fit right in. She'd dipped into the severance money Dr. Page had given her to cover the cost, but she knew she couldn't afford the extravagance, so later that day Charlie helped her put several pieces of her porcelain Lladro figurine collection up for sale on eBay to replenish her bank account.

It hurt her heart to do it. She loved her Lladro, but she also loved putting food on the table for her growing boys and keeping their house heated. Something had to give.

Finally, with time moving at a glacial pace, Bunny arrived in the gravel parking lot at the Rustic Woods Nature Center twenty minutes early, looking like she was ready to hike the Appalachian Trail with Grizzly Adams.

Barb was right, the boots were chunky. They felt like weighted moon boots. She met a young woman on her way to the entrance, who introduced herself as another naturalist. As Bunny walked alongside her new co-worker, she was mortified when she tripped over her own feet.

The young naturalist was apparently the first employee besides Bunny to arrive. She unlocked the main door to let them both in, and, unsure of quite what to do, Bunny decided to take her place at the reception desk while waiting for the frizzy-haired Abigail to arrive.

New boss, new job, and Tate Kilbourn. Her nervous energy was revved so high, she was probably burning a thousand calories a minute. She tried to keep busy by taking note of her new station. The phone system was similar, but not identical, to the one at Dr. Page's. Hopefully she'd learn it easily. Computer monitor. Much larger and newer than the one that Dr. Page had supplied. That was nice. She put her fingers on the keyboard. The fit was good.

She opened the top drawer on the right-hand side of the desk. It was a disorganized mess of rubber bands, paper clips, sticky note pads, scissors and more. The second drawer contained a gem—operating instructions for the phone system. She was reading the "Getting Started" chapter when she heard footsteps in the main hallway.

A moment later, Abigail appeared with a large, flowery tote thrown over one shoulder. She stopped and gave Bunny a queer look. "Can I help you?"

Surprised by the woman's reaction, Bunny froze. For a panicked moment she thought maybe she'd misunderstood the call on Friday. "Today was supposed to be my first day, right?"

Abigail's spine straightened, and the creases on her face relaxed. "Ms. Bergen?"

"Yes..."

The woman shook her head and continued moving toward Bunny. "I remembered you as blonde from the interview. My mistake."

"You weren't really mistaken. I was coloring my hair before, but now I'm going back to my natural look to fit in with the nature theme, you know." Bunny smiled, thinking her own little joke would ease the tension.

Abigail didn't crack a smile. She stared at her for a moment, then slapped her hand on the counter. "Yes. Well," the woman said with an abruptness that made Bunny jump. "Need to set my things down. Back shortly. Lots of paperwork to fill out." Abigail slumped again and, pointing her nose like a dog on a scent, walked with brisk determination down another hallway behind the reception desk.

Bunny turned to watch her new supervisor stride away. It was hard not to wonder how they were going to get along. Right now, Abigail felt like vinegar to Bunny's oil.

She returned her attention to the phone system user manual, but soon enough, she had the odd feeling she was being watched. She looked up again to find herself being inspected by a set of eyes staring through round wire-rimmed glasses. It was the small woman from the interview, whose name she'd forgotten.

Bunny was surprised to see that the woman wasn't just short, she was more like a miniature person. Her bulbous nose and round glasses hovered just above the tall countertop of the reception desk.

"I'm sorry," Bunny said. "I didn't hear you come up."

"That eez okay. People say I'm like stealth Russian spy drone. It eez dee shoes." Without a hint of a sound, she was scooting around the desk to show Bunny her feet. "You like?"

Bunny smiled to be nice. "Mm. Yes. They're very... white."

"Nurse shoes. Get dem online from nurse's site. You know—they have the scrubby clothes. And the shoes."

Actually, they did look very comfortable, so Bunny wasn't lying when she told the little woman that she'd like a pair for herself. The hiking boots were killing her feet at the moment. "I'm sorry," Bunny said, "I know we were introduced at the interview, but I've forgotten your name."

"Olga." Olga looked Bunny up and down in two swift shifts of her head. "You look different."

"I put a brown rinse in my hair. I'm going back to my natural—"

"No. I mean, yes, this ees obvious with the hair, but... you have different clothing choices. No pretty rings in your ears." The woman wiggled her own naked ear lobes to illustrate. "I always weeshed I did the holes for the rings."

"I wanted to dress appropriately. For the job, I mean."

"Why like this? You answer the phones, not climbing the mountains." She eyed Bunny's boots, winced, then leaned against Bunny's desk, settling in like an old buddy. "Me, I tell Abigail hire the blond lady. She dress up the place."

"Thank you."

Olga stepped over Bunny's attempt to express appreciation, waving her hand dramatically. "But she say she not hire bimbo. I say, 'Abigail, she not bimbo. That ees sexism, yes? Just because woman has blond hair, she ees bimbo.' But no, Abigail try to hire others first."

"Which others?"

"All others." She placed a hand on Bunny's shoulder. "All. But none willing," she rolled her eyes and blew out a hefty breath, "or able, to take dee job. One already have better offer, one decided to go back for the master's degree, and one—get thees—one come up on the search of criminal histories as being offender."

"Offender?"

"Sexual offender."

Bunny thought of the grimy man. "The man who wasn't dressed so well?"

Olga shook her head. "Woman with brief case. She was high school teacher who had much sex with many boy students. Bad lady. That man—he took good job with National Zoo."

"So I was the last choice?"

"Yes. I hate to break the news. But me, I like you. Think you bring color to the place. But not..." she made a sweeping motion in front of Bunny, "not dressed like this. Be yourself, yes?" She pushed herself from the desk where she'd been leaning and patted Bunny on the arm. Silently, Olga tore off down the same hallway as Abigail.

Bunny liked the little Russian lady, but was crushed to learn that she'd only been hired because none of the other applicants were eligible. A momentary thought of fleeing flashed through her mind. Fleeing before Abigail returned to train the bimbo she didn't think could answer phones.

Bimbo. That was almost worse than the word "skank." Well, maybe not, but the more she stewed, the more furious she became. Now angry rather than sad, and still very desperate to earn a living, Bunny bucked up, as her father would say, and grew some courage. She'd show Abigail that she wasn't a bimbo or a skank. She was a smart, responsible, organized woman capable of doing a whole lot more than just answering phones.

By the time Abigail returned with the promised paperwork, Bunny had taught herself the phone system, taken two calls and transferred them to the appropriate extensions, and cleaned up the mess in the top drawer.

The rest of the day went well, with one exception: She never saw Tate Kilbourn.

Bunny was ambivalent. On the one hand, she was extremely nervous to see him again, and on the other hand, she was extremely hopeful to see him again. But since she'd probably be seeing him every day anyway, it would be better to just start seeing him.

When Abigail had introduced her to the two junior naturalists who worked for Tate, Bunny casually asked where their boss was. She was told that he'd been in very early and left them a note that he was monitoring the lower branch of the creek system that fed the four lakes of Rustic Woods.

With just twenty minutes until closing time, Bunny was at her computer learning a data entry program, per Abigail's curt, but not unfriendly instructions.

Bunny could tell Abigail was surprised at her competence, despite the fact that the woman still wouldn't crack a smile.

Bent over, glancing from instruction book to monitor and back again to make sense of things, Bunny was deep in thought and never heard Tate approach the desk until he was practically breathing down her neck.

"That looks important, but I wonder if I could get your help for a minute."

She looked up, her heart beating faster at the sound of his rich, deep voice. Then she noticed the bloody hand he held toward her.

CHAPTER EIGHT

TATE WAS ANNOYED THAT THE first aid kit in his Nature Center truck was missing. He was even more annoyed that it was his own fault. Months earlier, he'd used it to patch up a worker who had been repairing the footbridge over Hunter Creek.

His best guess was that he left it behind that day.

When he sliced his right hand on a broken shard of glass while pulling a plastic bag from the reeds on the bank of Settlers Creek, he cursed loudly, but cursed even louder when he couldn't find the first aid kit. He wrapped his hand in a t-shirt he found on the floor of the truck and headed for the main office.

He'd purposely spent the entire day out walking the streams, pulling water samples and noting the condition of the banks and surrounding fauna. The air was cold enough to make the work unpleasant, but something about the way he'd reacted to Bunny Bergen made him want to stay away from the Center on her first day. Besides, the job had to be done. Might as well have been today.

He almost wondered if he'd cut his hand on purpose, though—subconsciously. He'd seen the glass there, for crying out loud. He wasn't usually that clumsy. He had felt a pull all day long—a pull to the Nature Center reception area. To see her there.

So when he walked in and saw her at the desk, focused so intently on the computer monitor, wearing a ridiculous turtleneck and fleece vest, hair tucked behind her delicate ears, he wanted to laugh. And he also knew instantly that the sweaty palms and churning gut he'd experienced at Fiorenza's wasn't a fluke. It was happening again. When she looked at him with her big green eyes and gasped at the blood on his hand, the urge to kiss her lips was so strong he had to take a step backwards.

"What did you do?" Bunny asked, pulling his hand toward her and carefully unwrapping the t-shirt bandage. A little crease formed between her eyebrows.

"Cut myself on some glass." He pointed his nose toward the lowest drawer near Bunny's feet. "I think there's a first aid kit in that drawer. Can you look?"

Still hanging onto his hand, she rolled her chair and pulled the drawer open with her other hand, retrieving the white box. She placed it on her desk, then examined his hand more closely. He both enjoyed and feared the sensations aroused by her tender, attentive care.

"This needs to be cleaned," she said, locking eyes with him again. "You don't want it to get infected. I see dirt here. Where did you find broken glass, anyway?"

He pulled his hand away. "In a stream. People party and throw their beer bottles into the water. You know." He shook his head, feeling self-conscious. "I'll wash it in the workroom, if you'll just hand me the kit."

Bunny stood and gave him a look. "Uh-uh. I saw that workroom—it's a mess. We'll do it in the kitchen sink where it's a little more sanitary, thank you very much. I'll help."

This was a woman far more confident than the one he'd seen at the interview just days earlier. He liked the take-charge attitude. And as he followed her to the kitchen, he liked her rear-end too. It seemed Bunny Bergen could wear anything and make it look good. Although those boots were...large.

Without speaking, Bunny turned the warm and cold water knobs, testing the temperature with her fingers. When she was satisfied, she took his hand and placed it under the warm flow.

He noticed, this time, that her own hands were shaking, and wondered why. "How was your first day? Abigail treating you all right?"

Bunny smiled and looked over her shoulder discreetly before speaking. "She's sort of blunt, but she was actually okay. I'll admit, she had me worried at first."

"You didn't make the mistake of calling her Abby, did you?"

"No," Bunny said, cleaning the wound with the liquid antibacterial hand soap. "She doesn't like it?"

"She doesn't have the best sense of humor."

"About what?"

Tate could see that Bunny hadn't made the connection yet. "Her last name..."

Bunny said her boss's name out loud. "Rode." Tate watched the wheels turn, then her face lit up as she rinsed the soap from his hand. "Abby Rode. Like the Beatles album," she whispered, smiling. "That's cute. I don't know why that should bother her."

She patted his hand with a clean dish towel she'd found in a drawer. She laid the towel on the counter next to the sink, then guided him to lay his hand, palm-up. Silently, she dressed the fairly long wound with antibiotic cream and a square bandage that just barely covered it from one end to the other.

Tate found himself mesmerized by her long fingers and the soft skin of her hands. He lifted his gaze to her ears and realized they were flaming red. The elegant line of her neck enticed him and he noticed that her hair smelled like vaguely like strawberries. He imagined burying his face in that neck and relishing the scent.

She patted down the edges of the bandage and stepped back. "You're fixed." Her smile was hesitant, and she tucked her head into her shoulders just a little. "I've taken my boys to the ER more times than I can count for stitches. I'm sure that cut doesn't need any. Of course, I'm not a nurse, just a mom."

"No, it's great." He examined the fine job she'd done. He bobbed his head, suddenly feeling awkward and without anything to say that didn't sound stupid. "Thank you," he finally managed to mutter.

Several strands of hair had come loose from behind her ear and fallen over her face. She tucked them back shyly.

She was opening her mouth to say something when Abigail's head poked through the open door, perma-frown pasted to her face. "I'm out of here. Bunny, if you're the last one to leave, make sure both back and front doors are locked and set the alarm just I like I showed you. Can you manage that?"

"I can," Bunny said. "Have a nice night."

Abigail didn't respond. She just turned and left in her usual abrupt manner.

Tate leaned over to confide a secret in hushed tones. "That's why I call her Crabby Abby."

Bunny muffled a laugh with her hand. "Not to her face, I hope!"

"Of course not." He smiled.

"I think she's just misunderstood," Bunny said, in what Tate took to be a very sincere thought.

He was touched by her kindness toward someone most people just considered grumpy. For a moment, he felt a little ashamed of himself.

An awkward silence fell between them. Tate thought of a million things to say, but rejected them all for one reason or another.

Finally, bobbing her head a couple of times, Bunny retreated toward the door. "I think it's almost closing time," she said. "I'd better go through the closing procedure list that she gave me."

"Sure. Right. Thank you again." Remembering the first-aid kit, Tate grabbed it and snapped it closed. "Don't forget this," he said just before she disappeared through the door.

"Oh! Thanks." She took the kit, her hands shaking again. "Um. Speaking of closing—will you be here much longer? I can wait until you leave to lock up."

"Actually, I'm just getting something from my office and heading out. You won't have to wait. I'll go out the back door—my car is parked in the back lot."

"Okay. See you tomorrow, I guess."

He nodded.

By the time he'd climbed into the front seat of his own blue Ford pickup, Tate was painfully aware of his heart pounding out of his chest, of the sweat on his palms and the back of his neck. He'd dated a few women over the years, but no one had made him feel this way since Jill.

His cell phone jingled in his coat pocket. He looked to see who was calling—Colt. He answered. "Hey buddy, what's up?"

"Kilbourn. Just checking in to see if the information we gave you was reliable. Were you able to talk to your brother?"

"Truthfully, haven't tried it yet. Long story."

"I get it, man. Family can be tough to deal with."

"Something like that." Tate wondered if he dare ask what was on his mind. Asking would make things more real. He might be forced by his own inquiry to go down a road he wasn't sure he was ready to explore.

"Well, listen Kilbourn, if you—"

As if controlled by a force other than reason, Tate interrupted his friend. "Hey, I was wondering..."

"Yeah?"

"How well do you know Bunny Bergen?"

CHAPTER NINE

By Thursday of her first week, Bunny felt like she was settling into the swing of her new job. She arrived early every morning, turned on all the lights, and set the Center's stereo system looping through a series of nature-themed music CDs. She'd learned which types of calls were forwarded to various people and which she could answer herself.

She'd taken Olga's advice and added a little spice back into her attire. Today she wore the flannel shirt with only the two top buttons unfastened, gold hoop earrings, which pleased Olga greatly, a wide, fancy belt to add some oomph, and low but very comfortable loafers.

The shoes weren't as quiet as Olga's stealth nurse's slippers, but they felt like a piece of heaven compared to the colossal hiking boots.

In the spirit of being a self-starter, Bunny paid special attention to the schedule for preschool field trips presented by the two junior naturalists, Lydia and Ross. Every time a group returned from a tour around the Center grounds, Bunny was waiting with cups of hot cocoa. She loved seeing the smiles on the children's faces as she told them to sit in the Nature Cove near the gas fireplace for their treats.

There, Lydia and Ross finished up their time with the kids, talking about the native wildlife indigenous to Virginia and demonstrating with both live and stuffed animals.

Later, Bunny was pleased when Lydia went out of her way to thank her for the extra touch of the hot cocoa.

"You have no idea how much that helped," Lydia told her. "By the end of a presentation, those kids can get antsy in the pantsy, but the hot chocolate kept them nice and quiet." She put a hand on Bunny's arm. "And they just loved you!"

"I adore children," Bunny admitted. "My favorite volunteer job when my boys were at Tulip Tree Elementary was reading to classes in the library."

"Feel free to help out in the future. We can use it." The young woman smiled.

Bunny used the moment to ask Lydia about Tate. She hadn't seen him since she'd dressed his cut on Monday night. "Hey," she said, trying to sound low key. "Some calls have been coming in for Tate, but he's not picking up, so I just forward them to his voicemail. Do you know where he is?"

Lydia rolled her eyes. "Tate is kind of a loner. It doesn't surprise me he didn't leave you a note or call you. He decided at the last minute to attend a conference at George Mason University. It ends today, so I guess he'll be back tomorrow, maybe."

"He's your boss, right?"

"And he's great as bosses go, trust me. As long as we do our job, he stays out of our hair. He's a cool guy—just quiet. Keeps to himself. Speaking of sending calls to voicemail," Lydia added, "I'm going out to start working on the bluebird houses. I need to clean them and do any repairs before spring bites me in the butt."

"I'll send any calls to voicemail," Bunny told her.

"Have them call my cell phone if it sounds urgent."

"Will do." Bunny really liked Lydia and Ross. They were far nicer than anyone at Dr. Page's dental office. Tomorrow she might consider asking them if she could join them for lunch. They usually ate at their desks, but she could hear them from down the hall, laughing and having a good time.

As for Tate Kilbourn, Bunny couldn't get him out of her mind. She kept thinking of how warm and firm his calloused hand had felt in her own when she helped clean that horrible cut. She hoped he hadn't noticed how badly her hands were shaking or the flush that had crept up her neck.

That night, after Michael had gone to bed and Charlie was finishing up homework in his room, she poured herself a glass of wine and went through her high school yearbook again, the one from her sophomore year, when Tate Kilbourn was a senior with whom she was madly in love.

Tate hadn't been the most popular guy in school, but he was well-known and well-liked. She turned to the group picture for Spanish Club. Tate was in the front row with the same dark hair, but longer and less tame. No beard yet. And the smile. That smile, that he willingly gave anyone who passed him in the hall, was what tugged at her heart and made her weak-kneed. He was the boy of her dreams; she had wanted to be the girl of his. But he was a senior, and she was that silly sophomore sitting in the back row of the Spanish Club picture, staring at him like some crazed goon through ugly glasses.

Flipping a few more pages, another club photo—Ski Club. Tate in the front row again as Vice President, same seductive smile. And Bunny, staring at him again from the second row from the back. She'd never skied a day in her life. She had signed up for a ski trip with the club, only to come down with a horrible case of the flu the day before.

She flipped a few more pages. Prom. She'd gone with her gay friend, Roger, wearing her new contact lenses. She knew Tate would be there with his girlfriend, the nearly perfect Wendy Little, but rumors had been floating around that she was dumping Tate right after prom since she had her sights on a football player from Virginia Tech.

That football player wound up crashing the prom, and Wendy Little spent the entire night glued to him, leaving poor Tate wandering the fringes of the dance floor like a lost puppy.

Roger had prodded Bunny to ask Tate for a dance—a bold move for shy Bunny. Buckling herself into a rocket and being shot to the moon would have been less scary than asking Tate Kilbourn to dance.

But she did it. With her insides all a jitter, her skin breaking out in hives, she asked Tate Kilbourn to dance. And to her surprise and delight, he actually said yes.

Only, once they walked onto the dance floor, the song changed from fast to slow. She still remembered the song: "More Than Words." Panicked, she had been ready for him to walk away. But he didn't. Without any hesitation, he pulled her to him.

As she looked into his amazing deep brown eyes, she was both thrilled and terrified. She didn't know if she should talk, and if she did her voice might shake so horribly it would reveal her secret love for him.

"You're Deena's sister, right?" he had asked her.

Bunny could only nod. Ironically, the song they danced to was about words, and yet she had none.

Her silence didn't daunt Tate. "She's in my physics class," he had offered.

Bunny nodded again and smiled, at least. She really didn't want to be talking about her demon older sister. Her hand slipped from his shoulder down to his upper arm, and she got a rush from the form of his bicep. She'd rather be talking about his arms, his eyes, his smile, his breath that smelled like Tic Tacs. Cinnamon Tic Tacs.

She had known he'd been accepted to the University of Virginia, but that wasn't so far away. She'd thought of asking him if he wanted to see a movie sometime, get some ice cream, see where this magic might lead. Maybe she could write to him while he was away at college, and she would be here when he came home during breaks.

Yes, she vividly remembered all of those thoughts passing through her mind while they danced, but speaking none of them. He would laugh at her silliness. Instead, she said, "I couldn't make the ski trip. I was throwing up." She moaned, even upon the recollection. Once the words were out of her mouth, she had nearly died from embarrassment.

But he didn't laugh at her. Thank God. Instead he said, "That's too bad. Maybe next year." They danced the rest of the song in silence, Bunny not daring to hold his gaze, but instead, staring at his shoulder and his dark wavy hair that fell just above the wonderful curve of his neck. Or she watched other dancers. Many snuggling like lovers, their bodies swaying as one.

When the song ended, Tate and Bunny pulled away naturally. She stared awkwardly at the ground.

"Thank you, Bunny," Tate said. "For the dance."

She looked up, surprised and elated that he knew her name. Then she did something completely out of character. Without a forethought, she took his hand in hers. "I'm sorry about Wendy," she said.

He gave her hand a squeeze and walked away, through the doors of the party room and out of her life. She'd seen him in the halls a few times before school ended for summer and once at the Rustic Woods Summer Jamboree where he caught her eye and smiled, but after he went to college, she'd never seen him again. She heard through the grapevine that he had stayed in Charlottesville the full four years and then moved out of the state afterward, but that was the extent of her knowledge.

She'd gone on to other crushes and had a real boyfriend by the end of her own senior year. And of course there were men in college, her husband, and Russ, the firefighter, but none of them ever remained as strongly attached to her heart as the boy she'd barely known—Tate Kilbourn.

Bunny pulled herself from the recollection of the night that happened so, so many years ago. She flipped pages until she found the senior photos and zeroed in on Tate's portrait. He'd always looked good, but he wore a suit with brilliance. Brown eyes sparkled from the page and that smile, wide and natural, made her heart melt. Below, his accomplishments were listed: National Honor Society, Football, Baseball, Spanish Club, Ski Club, Nature Club, Voted Most Likely to Save the World.

Tate Kilbourn had been an active guy. An outgoing guy. A guy whose smile captured people and wouldn't let go.

What had happened since high school to turn this social person into a man who preferred to be alone? He had a daughter—she'd met her at Fiorenza's. Very pretty and very sweet. She knew that the girl was playing opposite Charlie in the high school musical, but Charlie wasn't the biggest talker in the world. She could only imagine that if she asked him about the girl's father, he'd roll his eyes and say, "How should I know?" Yet, she sure would like to know why he had a daughter, but didn't wear a wedding ring.

Bunny closed the yearbook and put it aside, yawning. Her computer hummed across the room on its little desk, reminding her of something she wanted to do.

She sent a second email to the theater teacher, since she'd never received a reply to the first. She double-checked the email address from the website, just to make sure she hadn't made a mistake with the original.

Her latest note mentioned the same ideas—that she would love to help out in any capacity needed. Then she added that she knew putting on a play must involve a lot of work and that a theater teacher couldn't possible manage alone, so please let Bunny know how she could assist. "Have a wonderful day, Bunny Bergen, Charlie's mom." Send.

If Bunny didn't hear back, she would try calling. After all, Bunny thought, as a teacher and director of a school musical, the woman was probably very busy and too overwhelmed to answer every email she received.

CHAPTER TEN

THE CONFERENCE ON PRESERVING VIRGINIA'S natural wildlife had been mildly informative. Tate wasn't sure if he was glad he had decided to attend. His choice had been prompted by a need to steer clear of Bunny Bergen for a few days. He knew he couldn't avoid her altogether, but hopefully a few days away would drain him of the insane desire that kept invading his thoughts like the bamboo roots he fought to contain in his backyard.

Yes, she was beautiful and sexy and everything any man would find attractive—that wasn't what scared him. What terrified him to the bone was the realization that his feelings transcended pure lust. Lust he could handle. But there was something about Bunny: an innocence and a sincerity that tugged at him. Made him think beyond lust and reminded him of the other L word, and that's what terrified him. It had been too long. He wasn't ready. At least, he didn't think he was ready.

Yet, despite the time and distance, while sitting in a stuffy conference hall taking notes on dwindling beaver populations, Tate found himself fantasizing about kissing those soft, pink lips, caressing the naked small of her back, and inhaling the strawberry scent of her shiny brown hair. But that's where the fantasy hit the breaks with a deafening screech. Admitting to himself, even in a fantasy, that he could feel this way again, unleashed a raging river of guilt. Accustomed to shutting off his feelings, Tate set his mind back on the lecture of the hour, pushing thoughts of Bunny behind a black screen—only to have her resurface later, taunting him, making him ache.

Maybe, he decided after several nights of restless sleep, he needed to face this thing, whatever it was, head-on. Because surely he couldn't continue hiding from her forever.

He arrived at work early and spotted her car in the parking lot. Wasn't hard—it was the only other car there. Instead of parking in the rear and entering through the back door, he parked next to her, and entered bravely through the front.

He'd play it cool. Professional. Not overly friendly, but not antagonistic either. He breathed a sigh of relief when he passed the empty reception desk. As he moved toward his office, his head turned instinctively to the kitchen where he caught sight of her rinsing something in the sink. Before he could turn away, she had spun around.

"Hi!" she said, her smile instant. "You're back. Was the conference good?"

He returned the smile, but controlled it consciously. *Remember, man, not too much.* "Uh, yeah. Good information." He tipped his head to her, his way to gesture a hello without saying the words. That was what cool guys did. "I'll, uh, be in my office if anyone calls."

"Okay." She continued to smile while drying a mug with a dishtowel. "I made a pot of coffee." She made a motion as if she was about to turn away from him, but then stopped and added, "Welcome back."

In his office, the red light on his phone blinked incessantly, a sure sign that he had voicemails to sift through. At least ten of them would be from George, asking him to report on the conference and to submit any receipts.

Tate set his briefcase down, his gaze focused on a large plastic white box on his desk. A first-aid kit. Balanced across the kit was a long pinching grabber like those used to pick up trash along roadsides and highways.

A pink sticky-note secured to the box read: *Use one so you won't need the other,* with a smiley face drawn underneath. Bunny hadn't signed her name, but Tate assumed it wasn't Crabby Abby. Crabby's handwriting wasn't nearly as feminine, and she'd probably never drawn a smiley face in her life.

Tate lifted the pincher, wrapped his fingers around the handle and squeezed. The prongs at the opposite end closed. He smiled. Lead naturalist of the Nature Center, and he hadn't thought to equip his own truck with standard equipment given to volunteers.

He released the pincher, then squeezed again. Release, squeeze, release squeeze. A mindless task to perform while trying to decide how to thank Bunny.

A voice in the doorway startled him. "Glad we don't shoot video of you on the job for aspiring young naturalists. The disappointment would be crushing."

Tate turned and glared at Abigail. No words were necessary.

"But," she continued, "it's good that you're here. I'm calling an emergency meeting. Eleven a.m. conference room."

"Last time I checked, you didn't have authority to call me to any meeting. Now, if you asked nicely..."

"George has authority." She held up a piece of paper, letting it dangle. "Do you need to see the memo?"

Tate pulled his chair from under the desk and, turning his back to her, sat down. "See you at eleven. With bells on." He grabbed the receiver from its cradle and punched the red button to play back his messages.

One of his thirteen messages was from a woman who wanted to rent the picnic pavilion for her son's graduation. She'd been given his name as the contact to get that done. Unfortunately, picnic pavilion rental fell under Bunny's job description.

He was used to receiving these sorts of inquiries. Several times a year he handled phone calls, all from women, seeking to rent the pavilion. The pavilion was a hot commodity for graduation parties, so he decided rather than handling this one over the intercom with Bunny, he'd better talk to her about it in person. Give her a heads-up.

She was on the phone when he got there, so he hung out in front of her desk, resting an arm on the high counter top.

She smiled at him while she talked into the phone. "Mm, hm," she said. "I'll be sure to tell her. I'm sure she will find that idea very interesting, Mrs. Pichoff." Bunny nodded, then shrugged at Tate. "Yes. Yes. Call any time. We *love* your suggestions." She shook her head at Tate, which caused him to snicker out loud. "Okay. You take care of yourself, Mrs. Pichoff and think about seeing a doctor for that stomach ache if it doesn't go away. Bye-bye." She hung up the phone, giggling.

"You are far kinder toward Ethel Pichoff than our last receptionist."

"She just wants someone to talk to, the poor thing. Of course, I've only had to deal with her for five days now. The last receptionist was someone named Jenny, right? How long was she here?"

He shrugged. "Don't know. She was working here when I started last summer." He paused, captivated by the green of Bunny's eyes. It was the green of fresh new leaves sprouting from an ash tree in the spring.

He remembered the note in his hand. "I, uh...the picnic pavilion." He handed the piece of paper to Bunny. "This woman wants to rent it for a party in June."

She took the paper from him, her smile dropping and concern washing across her face. "Was this in your voicemail? I'm so sorry. I don't know why I forwarded it to you."

"No, no. It's not your fault. It happens. Which is why I, uh, came up here. Feel free to screen my calls—you know, double check before sending them back. You can just ask them if they're inquiring about renting the picnic pavilion."

Bunny tilted her head. "I don't understand. Was handling rentals ever part of your job?"

"No."

"But people call and ask specifically for you when they want to rent? That's strange."

"Yeah. Strange. Anyway..." He let the last word dangle only because his mouth seemed to be at odds with his brain.

Bunny glanced at the paper in her hands, and then a smile crept across her face. "Are they usually women?"

Tate felt his face flush. Thank goodness for the beard. He hoped it concealed his embarrassment. "Who knows? I'm not sure I pay attention."

"Hey," Bunny said, sitting straighter in her chair. "Your daughter is in the school musical, right?"

Relieved that the conversation had changed gears, Tate's shoulders relaxed. He nodded.

"I've been sending emails to the theater teacher—Charlie said she's the director—but she's not responding. I had a question for her."

"Why don't you just ask her at the meeting tonight?"

"What meeting?"

"There's a meeting for parents of the cast and crew. There was an email."

Bunny frowned, then grabbed a piece of paper from the printer tray and a pen from the holder in front of her. "When? Where?"

"Seven. Hang on, it might be seven thirty." He pulled his cell phone from his pocket, using his thumb to scroll. "Here it is. Seven o'clock in the auditorium."

"Thank you." Bunny's face brightened. "I don't know why I didn't get that email. Are you going?"

"It's mandatory. Willow says the teacher is headstrong. That's my word, not Willow's. She was a little more colorful."

"Mandatory. Huh." Bunny slumped a little in her chair. "I'm glad I asked you then."

Olga's head popped up beside his arm, and she peered over the counter at Bunny.

"Deed you hear about emergency meeting in conference room?" she asked Bunny. Then, without waiting for an answer, she bent her head way back and eyeballed Tate through her round glasses. "You?"

Tate and Bunny nodded.

Olga's frown deepened. "Ack!" And off she bounded, silently down the hallway—all three feet of her.

Olga's departure gave Tate the perfect momentum to get his butt moving as well. "I'd better prepare for," he jumped into an imitation of Olga's Russian accent, "Emergency meeting!"

Bunny saluted him and chuckled. "You don't want to arrive unprepared."

He gave the desk counter a little pat. "Nope." On his way to his office, he stopped at the kitchen to pour himself a cup of coffee. As he did so, he realized he was having trouble holding the mug still—his hand was shaking that badly.

CHAPTER ELEVEN

BUNNY ARRIVED AT THE SCHOOL auditorium a few minutes before seven and took a seat three rows back from the front. She was still shaken up from an argument with Michael—he wanted to go to his father's house even though it wasn't Richard's weekend. This had been a recurring argument in her house lately, and she wondered if Richard was busy making trouble for her again.

A few parents had arrived already, mostly mothers. Two women she recognized sat in the row in front of her a few seats to her right. She knew them from her days attending PTA meetings at the elementary school, but their names escaped her.

One of them turned to scan the back of the auditorium, and when she did so, caught Bunny's gaze. Bunny smiled and offered a tiny wave, but the woman offered nothing in return except to show Bunny the back of her head.

Bunny's smile dropped. She shifted in her chair, stomach knotting at the obvious snub. Okay, she told herself, maybe it wasn't a snub. Maybe the woman didn't remember Bunny.

Bunny crossed her legs and tried to appear comfortable in the chair and in her own skin. Nonchalantly looking this way and that, she strained for a glimpse of Tate Kilbourn. If he was here, she hadn't spotted him yet. She checked the time on her cell phone and watched as a few more women and one man—not Tate, darn it—took seats. Some sat in pairs, some alone.

After a good forty people or so had arrived, Bunny heard a heavy metal door slam shut, followed by clacking heels. The clacking ceased when the feet in the small black heels hit carpeting. The owner of the shoes was a tall woman with long black hair and very pale skin. She bore a distressing resemblance to Morticia Addams, a resemblance that was reinforced by the long black dress she wore. She cradled a stack of notebooks and papers in her arms as she approached the front of the auditorium.

She placed the stack of items onto the stage and, wasting no time, turned to the awaiting audience of parents and clapped her hands three times. The sharp sound reverberated through the cavernous room, capturing everyone's attention and silencing them instantly.

Bunny was impressed, but a little frightened at the same time. Brusque people had that effect on her.

"Good. Thank you." The woman looked from one side of the auditorium to the other. "We have little time and much to cover. For those of you who don't know: I am Ms. Steffler."

The woman proceeded to grab the papers from behind her and walk up the nearest aisle, passing thin stacks to parents and asking them to take one and pass the rest down their row. Since Bunny was on the aisle, she took the offered handouts.

"Thank you," she said, attempting to catch the woman's attention with a smile.

Again, the smile was ignored. In fact, Bunny was ignored altogether, since the woman never bothered to look at her.

Ms. Steffler was busy frowning toward the back. "You people back there," she said, raising her voice as she shoved the papers in Bunny's face. "Please come and take these seats closer. I don't feel like shouting to be heard this evening."

Bunny followed directions, standing to reach several seats to her right and pass the handouts to a father sitting there, stone-faced. *People sure are cranky tonight*, Bunny thought. *Would it hurt someone to smile just a little bit?*

As parents migrated to seats near the front, the teacher began preaching the high expectations she had for the cast and crew, as well as her expectations for the parents. "Mothers, Fathers, Guardians," she bellowed, raising her hands like a reverend before a Sunday service. "You set the example for your student. I count on you to make sure they arrive at rehearsal on time, that they are getting the rest they need at night, and the proper nutrition during the day."

She shifted her hard stare from one side of the room to the other with a good deal of dramatic flair. "I cannot be expected to work with teenagers who show up ten minutes late, narcoleptic and ravenous. I am not their parent, *you* are. Do your job, and I will do mine."

Hmm, thought Bunny, *I guess in college she majored in Theater Arts and minored in Fascist Studies. Or maybe it was the other way around.*

Bunny raised her hand to ask about volunteering. The time seemed right—Ms. Steffler was talking about parent responsibilities, after all.

The teacher seemed not to notice, so Bunny held her hand up higher, adding a little wave.

Apparently the wave worked. Ms. Steffler heaved a sigh and directed a chastising glare right at Bunny. A glare that went on for six long seconds. Bunny knew because she counted while fighting back the urge to vomit.

Ms. Steffler then spoke slowly and succinctly. "I'm sorry. Possibly the email was not clear enough: this is not a Q and A."

The words sizzled in Bunny's ears with the tight, patronizing tone of a superior addressing a dimwitted inferior. Her face flushed, and her fists tightened just as they had when Lois told her that Broom Hildie had called her a skank. Why did people have to be so nasty?

She bit her lip and nearly choked down her next comment, but somehow it slipped out anyway. "I didn't get that email. In fact, I've sent you two emails, which you still haven't answered." Her voice cracked over each word. But, since she'd gone this far, she may as well go all the way. "I'm not sure how a person should get a question answered. I only wanted—"

"Your name please?" the woman interrupted.

Was she going to send Bunny to detention or something? "Bergen. Bunny Bergen. I'm Charlie—"

Again, interrupted. "Ms. Bergen," the teacher said with stinging condescension. She placed her hands together as if praying and paused again for the effect. "It was each student's responsibility to supply me with at least one parent email address. And each day, even though it goes against my beliefs, I reminded them to get me that email address. Ms. Bergen—of the fifty-six students in the cast and crew of the spring production of *Kiss Me, Kate*, one," she held up her index finger in case Bunny was too doltish to understand. "Only one did not give me a parent email address."

Another dramatic pause.

Bunny's heart thumped hard and fast.

"Ms. Bergen," Morticia the Witch continued, "the person to whom you should be speaking is your son." The woman had icy blue eyes that matched her heart, and she locked them onto Bunny's. "But, Ms. Bergen, since you seem preoccupied with these emails, don't keep me on pins and needles. Tell me your concern."

Bunny cleared her throat, aware of the many eyes on her. "Volunteering. I just wanted to offer myself as a volunteer." Her voice quavered horribly, and she prayed for the moment this would all be over.

"All emails or phone inquiries regarding parent volunteer opportunities were forwarded to my volunteer coordinator who should be arriving momentarily. I imagine if you exercise patience, Ms. Bergen, she will contact you in due time. Now, is that all?"

Bunny began to nod but found herself jolted by another metal door slamming, followed by more clicking heels on the floor.

A woman, who was shorter than Ms. Steffler, strode confidently toward the teacher, full of smiles. For the first time since starting her dictatorial lecture, the teacher allowed a broad smile to cross her own face.

Bunny wasn't smiling. Bunny was fuming.

"Parents!" the teacher said in a grand and happy tone, raising one arm to greet the other woman. "Please meet our parent volunteer coordinator. I'm also pleased to call her friend. Mrs. Hildie Page."

CHAPTER TWELVE

NOT ONE FOR SOCIALIZING, TATE had purposely arrived at the school auditorium five minutes after seven. Immediately put off by Ms. Steffler's manner, he ignored her order to move toward the bow of her slave ship.

Instead, he remained firmly attached to the wall on which he leaned near the rear double doors. The location gave him both a good view and a quick get-away.

It took him less than ten seconds to locate the back of Bunny's head. She sat alone, one seat in from the aisle, three rows back from the stage. He could easily have done as the teacher commanded and slipped into the empty seat beside Bunny. The proximity would have been a pleasant one. But he stayed put. Felt safer that way.

The morbidly dark woman with the superior attitude droned on while Tate scanned the handout that contained detailed lists of dates for rehearsals, set production schedules, costume production schedules, and showtimes.

He had no idea a play required so many different types of rehearsals—book rehearsal, song rehearsal, choreography rehearsals, and orchestra rehearsals. Book rehearsal meant nothing to him. Nor did the term "dark," which he saw listed on two different nights on the showtime schedule.

He flipped through the many stapled pages, scanning for a glossary of terms when Bunny's voice caused him to look up.

"I didn't get that email," she said.

It didn't take Tate long to realize that she was addressing Steffler, whose tone rose to heightened levels of domination when Bunny questioned her accessibility. Steffler was the alpha-dog, and she intended for Bunny to submit.

Tate was torn between the desire to urge her to fight back and throwing a heavy punch to the teacher's kisser himself. He watched other parents whisper to each other while Steffler stared Bunny down.

He had taken two steps forward when a pair of doors opened to the side of the stage. Who should enter but Hildie Page, waving her manicured hands and flashing her bleached white smile. Those teeth were so big she looked like she belonged on the Kennedy family tree.

Tate rolled his eyes. His forward motion stopped. He had planned to take that seat next to Bunny as a show of moral support, but the arrival of Hildie Page changed his mind.

Now he ran escape scenarios through his head, hoping she hadn't zoned in on him yet. He could slip into the seat to his right and slump down. Or back slowly toward the doors in the rear.

A late arrival made a significant amount of noise opening and closing those rear doors that had once seemed so appealing to Tate. The commotion captured Hildie's attention, and when she lifted her surgically enhanced eyes, she spotted Tate.

Tate gulped. His getaway plan was foiled, and he knew it.

"Tate Kilbourn!" she gushed, raising her arm to announce him to the room. "Tate Kilbourn, come down here!"

He saw Bunny spin around at the mention of his name. He shrugged at her, then rebuffed Hildie's request, waving his hands and shaking his head. "No, no," was all he managed to say. He wanted to say more but being a gentleman, decided to leave it at "No," and took two steps backward.

"Parents," Hildie shouted to the room. "Help me thank Mr. Kilbourn for offering to head-up the set production of *Kiss Me, Kate*! Give him a hand!"

All eyes were on Tate, but all he really saw was Bunny.

She watched him, clapping with less enthusiasm than the other parents, most of whom were turned in their seats. applauding.

Why were they clapping anyway? Because he finally relented after endless phone calls and two uninvited trips to his house from Hildie Page?

Offered? No. Tate hadn't offered. He'd been railroaded by Rustic Woods' expert on facelifts and spray tans. She'd done everything but hump his leg when she "ran into him" at the Java Hut two days earlier.

To avoid further harassment, he'd agreed to be the parent volunteer in charge of set building. And he'd regretted that promise every second of every minute since. Not that he didn't like the idea of helping the kids out.

He did. He actually looked forward to that part of his duty. But the thought of dealing with Hildie Page for the next six weeks made him sympathize with young men who scrambled across the borders to Canada to avoid the draft.

By agreeing, he'd hoped to get Hildie off his back. But when the phone calls increased in number and the emails began filling his inbox at exponentially increasing rates, he realized that the horror had only begun.

Tate took his time getting to his pick-up truck, hoping to spot Bunny.

The student parking lot at Rustic Woods High was large and filled nearly to capacity. While passing the gym on his way out after the parent meeting, the reason became clear. A well-attended basketball game was still going strong. Through the sea of cars, he'd never spot Bunny's vehicle, especially in the dark.

Once beside his faithful blue Ford, he slipped the key slowly into the lock while keeping one eye out for Bunny and the other peeled for hormone-heavy Hildie. He'd have fled long ago, but he felt a strong tug toward Bunny. He wanted to talk to her and see how she'd weathered the gale force of Steffler's attack. Maybe he could offer to take her for a drink at Roger's Grill in the Muir Lake Center. Just a drink between friends, he'd make it clear, to toast her bravery.

But if Bunny was out there, he wasn't locating her, and each passing moment increased the risk of being zoned in on by Hildie. He climbed into the truck, closed the door, put the key in the ignition, and pumped the gas pedal twice. As he was about to start the motor, he caught sight of a tall woman through his windshield. She wore a long coat that looked like the one he'd seen hanging on the back of Bunny's chair.

He hesitated. When the woman walked under a streetlight, he knew—it was Bunny. His heart beat faster. The thought of talking to her here, outside of work, had seemed easy enough when it was just an idea. Actually making the move—that was harder.

Twice, he reached for the door handle only to pull his hand back. She was opening her own car door. It was now or never.

Tate yanked the key from the ignition and pushed his door open in one swift move. She was twenty, maybe twenty-five feet away. With one foot on the ground and one still poised in his truck, he called across the cars. "Bunny!"

She turned. There was no backing out now. He'd started this party, time to keep it moving. He pulled his other foot to the ground, slammed the door shut, and headed toward her.

She didn't come to meet him halfway, but remained standing under the light next to her car. Her hair framed her face, and the light fell in such a way that her innocent beauty shone brighter than usual. She didn't smile. She almost looked afraid.

"Hi!" Tate's breath fogged the cold air as he spoke.

"You didn't tell me you were a parent volunteer," Bunny said. He couldn't tell if it was an accusation or just a statement of fact.

He shrugged. "I didn't exactly apply for the job, let's put it that way." Instead of allowing an awkward lull, he steamrolled through. "That Steffler is a piece of work, isn't she?"

"That's one way to describe her, I suppose. I can think of other words, but I try not to use them in public."

Tate laughed, but Bunny didn't join him. And she still wasn't smiling. He flailed, wondering what to say next. He could mention that his daughter had a crush on Charlie. Then, of course, he'd have to face the wrath of a teenage girl day in and day out. Scratch that.

He could tell her how well she'd withstood Steffler's veiled attack, but every way he considered phrasing it sounded patronizing. Scratch that.

He could tell her that he'd thought of nothing but her since he last saw her sitting at her desk with the phone to her ear, brushing the hair away from her eyes, looking like the sexiest damn receptionist he'd ever seen. Definitely scratch that.

The drink at Roger's Grill seemed like the best option by far.

"Hey," he said, revving up some courage to spit out the invitation. "Would you, uh, I mean—"

Even before Tate said the word "you" he could tell from Bunny's expression that something was wrong.

"Tate Kilbourn!" Hildie's voice echoed across the parking lot. His eyes shut on a wince. When he opened them again, Bunny was halfway into her car.

Tate heard the clacking of Hildie's heels on the macadam as Bunny slammed her door shut and turned her engine over. He stepped back and looked into her window, hoping to get some sort of take on what had just happened.

Bunny threw him a little wave and *whoosh*, she was gone, her old car chugging out of the lot.

He had the feeling she would have taken that thing out at hyper-speed if she could have.

He braced himself as the clicking heels drew nearer.

CHAPTER THIRTEEN

UNNY ENTERED HER HOUSE FROM the garage, slamming the door hard. Still fuming from the public humiliation incurred at the hands of Ms. Steffler, Theater Teacher from Hell, she marched upstairs and knocked twice on Charlie's bedroom door before letting herself in.

He was in bed, propped by pillows against the headboard, reading a book.

"Why didn't you give Ms. Steffler my email address?"

"What?"

"My email address. She asked for it several times, and you didn't give it to her. And don't tell me that you don't know her name by now."

He shrugged. "I thought I did." He smiled. "Take your coat off and stay a while."

"It's not funny, Charlie. The woman embarrassed me in front of all of those parents."

"She's pretty harsh."

"Harsh? She's Elvira with whips and chains."

"Who?"

"Never mind." She tore her coat off. "Harsh. She's harsh. Cruel. Inhuman. That's what she is. Inhuman."

"Mom. Settle down. I have to deal with her, you don't."

"All I wanted to do was volunteer."

"Don't worry about it. I'm sure they have plenty of volunteers."

"Who do you know with the last name Page?"

"You mean Nina Page?"

"What is she? Cast or crew?"

"She's, uh, the lead." He gave Bunny a look like she should know this. "She always gets the female lead."

That didn't surprise Bunny. Mommy probably saw to it. "What grade is she in?"

"Senior."

"Is she nice?"

He shrugged again. "I don't really know her that well. She's popular. Why?"

Bunny sighed. She didn't want to lay the Broom Hildie saga on him. She always tried to keep her problems just that: her problems, not her kids'. "What's that?" She indicated the book he was reading.

"The play—I'm memorizing my lines. Trying anyway."

Bunny folded her coat over her arm. "I'll leave you alone, then."

She closed the door behind her, then knocked on Michael's door and opened it only to find a dark room. "Charlie!" she hollered, "do you know where Michael is?"

"Dad picked him up a little while ago. He said he texted you, and you said it was okay."

She pushed Charlie's door open again, not believing what he had just said. "Who? Who texted me?"

"Michael."

Trying to restrain her anger, Bunny pulled the door closed, stomped downstairs, marched to her phone and dialed.

A woman's voice picked up after three rings. "Hello?"

"I need a drink and an ear."

"My house is a disaster. How about I pick you up and we go to that new place—Roger's Grill."

"That's perfect."

"Give me ten minutes."

"Thanks, Barb."

Bunny and her friend with an ear, Barbara Marr, sat at a booth sipping very dry pinot grigio from tall wine glasses. They were awaiting their ordered desserts—Double Chocolate Sin for Barb and Peach Crisp a la Mode for Bunny. Bunny was looking forward to the crisp, but was desperate for the a la mode.

"I've seen Hildie Page's name on PTA emails," Barb said, "but I've never met her. I took the girls to see last year's school musical, though. Her daughter is talented, I have to say. She's a natural."

"Her mother doesn't look very natural." Bunny drummed her fingers on the table.

"What does she look like?"

"Big teeth."

Barb's eyes widened, and she tilted her head back. "Okay. Yeah, she was there the night we saw the play. Big hair? Looks like she lives at the plastic surgeon?"

"That's her."

"So Ms. Steffler and Hildie Page are friends? That seems an unlikely match. Steffler's..." Barb tipped her head while looking for the right word.

"Creepy?"

"Sure. That's a nice word. Callie took the theater class her freshman year and dropped it after day one. The woman gave her nightmares. In fact, she's the only woman I know who might actually be able to intimidate my mother."

Bunny laughed. Barb's mother was even taller than Bunny and possessed the intensity that could make a marine colonel shake in his boots.

Bunny raised her eyebrows as the waiter appeared, a dish in each hand. He placed her a la mode delight on the table. She dug in while Barb unwrapped her fork from the napkin sleeve.

"I have an interesting tidbit to share," Barb said, giving Bunny a sly smile before diving into her Double Chocolate Sin.

"Only share if it's good news. I can't handle any more bad news right now."

"It's good news, alright."

"Then please, share."

"A certain person that you know happened to be talking to Colt the other day, and that certain person asked about you."

Bunny put her fork down. Her stomach churned, and she was sure the a la mode wasn't to blame. "Tate?"

"Mr. Sexy Naturalist Guy himself."

"When?"

"Not sure. Colt mentioned it today, but I kind of got the idea it was a few days ago. Probably after we all saw each other at Fiorenza's, I'm guessing?"

"What was he asking?"

"Remember, this is Colt we're talking about. Take it with a grain of salt, but basically he said it sounded like Tate was fishing. Like he might be interested."

Bunny shook her head. "I'm not so sure."

"Of course he is. You're sweet, and you're gorgeous. And he, by the way, is as sinfully sexy as this dessert. I don't know what he's doing at the Nature Center. That man should be making action movies. Half-naked."

"Hildie Page is after him. Looks like the feeling is mutual."

"She's married!"

Bunny shrugged. "Affairs happen."

"You got this from the meeting tonight?"

"Oh yeah, she was all, 'Tate Kilbourn is our knight in shining armor, isn't he wonderful, give him a hand for helping our kids build the sets and stuff. Ooh, ah.'"

Barb was trying to keep her latest forkful of chocolate sin from spewing out of her mouth as she laughed at Bunny's imitation.

"Then she followed him out to the parking lot. Probably wanted to offer him a..." she lowered her voice to a whisper, "a hand of her own, if you know what I mean." Bunny's face flushed. She didn't usually talk dirty like that.

Barb laughed out loud, having successfully swallowed. "Bunny, you're too funny. Are you going to finish that peach crisp?"

Bunny shook her head and pushed the plate to her friend.

"Colt and Tate are friends," Barb said around a mouthful of peach crisp. "Colt has been helping him with some stuff, so I'll just have him dig a little more. Casually, you know."

Bunny and Barb sipped on their wine until the glasses were drained.

Bunny talked about her problems with Michael, and Barb talked about learning the ropes at the private investigative business. Howard, being retired FBI, was a valuable asset to Colt, but for Barb, the learning curve was tough.

Bunny thought it sounded very exciting, and she wished she was married to an ex-FBI agent and delving into the world of private investigation. Heck, she wished she were married. Then she thought about her problems with Michael and how horrible Richard had been lately. Marriage didn't seem very appealing when observed from the back end of a divorce.

They had paid their check and were scooting from their booth when Barb grabbed Bunny's arm. "Don't look now," she whispered while watching the entrance, "but we're about to have company." She lifted her eyebrows, smiled and waved to someone.

Ignoring the don't-look-now, Bunny turned while slipping an arm into her coat. Approaching them was none other than Colt Baron and Tate Kilbourn.

Oh, noodles. Bunny struggled to get her other arm into its sleeve, all while attempting to appear calm and collected and hopefully stunning.

Finally, her hand appeared at the end of the sleeve, and while the coat felt unusually tight, she stood straight and, having nothing better to do with her hands, clasped them in front of her.

"Curly!" Colt said, giving Barb a friendly punch to the arm. "Long time, no see, amiga."

Barb gave him a look. "It's been the longest four hours of my life."

Colt looked at his watch. "You can't count. It's been six, at least." He grinned, then leaned back on his heels. "Man, the four of us need to stop meeting like this. It's getting to be a habit."

Tate gave a quick nod and made a mild attempt at a smile. His hands were plunged into his coat pockets. "Funny."

Bunny forced a laugh and wondered whether it would look strange if she just ran out the door and waited for Barb there. Yeah. That would look strange. "Small world," she said. "I just can't seem to get away from this guy either. We work together too. And our kids are both in the school musical—Kiss Me, Tate."

She smacked her hand over her mouth, horrified. "Kate!" she sputtered in an attempt to undo the worst slip of the tongue ever. "*Kiss Me, Kate!*" She should have run when she had the chance. "The play is, uh, *Kiss Me, Kate.*" She emphasized the K in Kate, realizing the more she babbled, the worse it sounded.

Tate looked like he was trying hard to keep a grin under control, and Colt was eyeing him with a smirk.

That was it. She'd need to look for a new job now. "We should probably go, right, Barb?" She turned to grab her purse only to find that it wasn't there.

She sidestepped and looked in the seat where Barb had been sitting. "My purse! Do you see my purse?" She looked under the table in a panic. She *really* didn't need this right now. "I came in with it, right?" She looked to Barb for help. "Of course I did. I paid, so I must have had it."

Barb tapped her on the shoulder. "Um, sweetie, look under your coat. Actually, why don't you just take the whole thing off and try again. It's…"

It was on inside out. And she'd put it on over the purse that had already been thrown over her shoulder. That's why it felt so tight. She waved her hand to dismiss her ditzyness. "You know what, let's just go, Barb. I can…" Noodles! Her voice cracked again. "See you Monday, Tate. Bye, Colt." Bunny wanted to gallop out of the restaurant, but tried instead to make a graceful exit.

Who was she kidding? She'd already missed graceful by a long shot.

CHAPTER FOURTEEN

TATE'S KITCHEN TABLE WAS SWATHED in light, a gift from an early morning March sun. The first day of March. Gripping his coffee mug with both hands, he stared out the window, grateful that spring was just around the corner. The winter hadn't been too harsh, but then again, it wasn't over yet. He looked forward to a good warm day for taking Willow out in the canoe. They could go to Lake Muir, or maybe they would drive a little farther and paddle the Potomac.

And his gardens would need some tending. He had already ordered mulch, which would go down on the hosta and tulip beds, around the base cherry and dogwood trees, and under the butterfly bushes. He wondered though, if heading up the set-building crew for the school musical would cut deep into those plans.

He had already spent his entire Saturday locating and moving old scenery pieces from previous plays to his garage, where, he learned Friday night, most of the work would have to take place. Hildie had mentioned, almost as a slip of the tongue, that the school didn't have the room or tools for set building. That would have been information better offered up front, and he kicked himself for not thinking to ask the question.

Willow bounded into the kitchen, far more energetic than usual for a Sunday morning. She bent and planted a kiss on his bearded cheek. "Morning, Tater Tot."

"That's Tater Pop to you, my child." He watched suspiciously while she grabbed the coffee carafe and poured herself a cup. Not only was she awake, and apparently happily so, but she was dressed. "What time is it, anyway?"

She squinted at the digital display on their microwave. "Eight thirty-two." She pulled a bottle of flavored creamer from the fridge and poured a generous amount into her cup.

"A little early for your kind, isn't it?"

She took a seat next to him and slurped. "We're getting together to run lines at The Java Hut."

"Who is 'we' exactly?"

"A few of us."

"You're full of specifics today."

"You're beating around the bush today."

"I don't think it's me doing the beating, but okay, I'll go ahead and ask—will Charlie Bergen be there?" By her choice of attire—jeans and a frilly blouse instead of her usual sweatpants and Rustic Woods High School hoodie—he was pretty sure of the answer.

She smiled. "He would be one of the few. Yes."

"I think you need a chaperone. I'll go get dressed." He made a pretense of rising from his chair.

"Nice try, old man. I know you better than that." She slurped some more. "What do you have planned for today?"

He loved her, but the girl needed to learn the skill of drinking quietly. He raised his own cup. "Need to head over to the condo just to make sure all is well."

"Any offers yet?"

He shook his head. "But several people have been through according to the management, so hopefully soon. I'd like to have this done with."

Tate ran a hand through his yet unwashed hair. Months earlier, after a year or more of hounding from May and himself, Morton had agreed to purchase a retirement condo at Whispering Pines. Once Morton relocated to the condo, he'd intended to repair his large, empty house and put it up for rent. Days before the scheduled move, he'd become ill, and was soon diagnosed with stage four pancreatic cancer.

Logic would dictate that moving to the condo was more important than ever, but Morton would have none of it. If death was imminent, he decided he would rather go in the house he had owned most of his life. Selling the condo had become Tate's responsibility. The staff at Whispering Pines said the units usually went quickly, but winter was slow for everyone. He checked on the place once a week to pick up realtor's cards and to turn off lights and water faucets.

It seemed prospective buyers liked to turn faucets on to test them, but lacked the intelligence to realize that turning them off again was not only smart, but good manners.

"And Morty?" Willow asked.

"Yeah. I'll spend some time with him today. You should come."

"Okay. When?"

"Let's meet here at..." He looked at the microwave clock and did some mental calculations. "Two o'clock. You need a ride to the Java Hut?"

She shook her head. "Nina's picking me up." She popped out of her chair. "Speaking of which, I need to get ready."

He smiled. Willow looked plenty ready to him. He skimmed the cast list with his mind's eye. Nina. Nina. Oh, right. Nina Page. She was the lead. He hoped she wasn't anything like her mother. He took one more hefty swig from his cup, and then set about getting his own day moving.

Sunglasses still in place to block the beautifully bright day, Tate strode casually through the doors at Whispering Pines. The lobby was usually quiet, with a person or two at the desk making an inquiry and a few elderly residents sitting in the adjoining common room.

Today wasn't that day. Two women stood at the desk, one speaking frantically to Dan Baker, the facilities manager, who was holding a phone to his ear. His assistant, Nancy, stood beside him, her ear to another phone.

Tate pulled the sunglasses down on his nose to focus on the unfolding scene.

The frantic woman was Bunny Bergen.

Without thinking, he moved to her side. "What's wrong?"

Bunny turned in surprise. "Tate! What are you...?"

Dan Baker hung up the phone. "He's not answering."

"I know he's not answering," Bunny said in exasperation. "That's why I'm here. I even had Yetta text him, but he's not coming to the door. Something is wrong! You need to give me the key." Her voice rose several octaves.

Nancy covered the mouthpiece of her phone. "Mr. Kinkle is on the phone and says his father hasn't been reachable since Friday night," she said to Dan.

"Neither has mine," said the woman next to Bunny. "What's going on in this place?"

Bunny held her hand out across the desk. "Mr. Baker, just give me the key while you help these other people—"

The man shook his head. "You know I can't do that, Mrs. Bergen."

"You can't give the woman the key to her father's unit when there's obviously a problem?" Tate asked louder than he had intended.

"Mr. Kilbourn, this is between—" The phone rang, and the man looked at it briefly. "Nancy, answer that please." He ignored Tate and focused on Bunny. "This is an unusually busy Sunday," he said to her, "and I apologize for the inconvenience. As soon as things settle down, I will contact your sister—"

"Mr. Baker," Nancy interrupted, "I'm sorry, but, um, Roger Whitaker's daughter is on line two. She says her father isn't answering his phone, either. And I still have Mr. Kinkle holding on line one, worried about his father."

Tate could sense Bunny's fear and frustration. Her hands were balled into fists on the counter, and her face and ears as red as peppers. He placed his arm on the desk, leaned forward and spoke with forceful clarity. "Mr. Baker, I happen to know that you personally have authority to enter a resident's condo when the resident's life might be in danger. I suggest you exercise that authority with regard to Ms. Bergen's father right now—before your potential legal problems grow out of control."

"Mine too!" the other woman yelled. "I *do* have authority, and I want my father's key now!"

Nancy and Dan retreated to a back room and returned quickly. Dan, a set of keys in his hand, motioned to Bunny to follow him to the elevator. "Let's go."

Bunny followed, then turned to Tate. He thought she was going to thank him, but the fear in her eyes held a different plea.

"Shall I come?" he asked.

She nodded.

When the elevator didn't arrive quickly enough, the three of them took the stairs, two at a time, to the fourth floor. They stopped in front of apartment number 403, where Dan Baker fumbled with the keys until he finally picked one and unlocked both the deadbolt and doorknob.

The three of them shoved into the tiny entrance, and Bunny gasped.

Tate held her shoulders while maneuvering to see what had upset her.

Four elderly men lay unconscious—two on the couch, one on the floor face down and the last one in a reclining chair with his limbs sprawled every which way. Cans of Red Bull littered the place along with empty chip bags and pizza boxes.

He would have thought them dead until one of the men emitted a snore loud enough to wake the dead.

Bunny ran past the four men and disappeared into the bedroom. Tate heard her yelling, "Daddy, Daddy, are you okay?"

When Tate stepped into the living room and spied the gaming unit connected to the television, he couldn't suppress a laugh. Another man snored as Tate picked up a controller and pressed one of the buttons. The television awoke from its sleep mode, displaying the start screen for *Steel Warriors*, a popular video game pitting aliens against heavily armed soldiers. Tate had played the game himself at Colt Baron's house. He was impressed with Bunny's father.

He turned at the sound of an older woman's voice. "They're addicted," said the lady. "Play that damn game day and night. I keep sayin', 'DH you're wasting your life away with those crazy games.'" She looked around the room. "Man, they musta had a wild time last night, eh?"

Dan Baker flipped open his phone just as Bunny returned. "He's okay," she said, "but a little mad right now."

Tate heard the man holler from what must have been his bedroom. "Get the hell outta my house! I'll do what I want to do!"

Bunny winced.

"Nancy," Dan said into his phone. "Tell the concerned relatives that we've found their fathers. They're alive and well. Over stimulated maybe, but well."

CHAPTER FIFTEEN

UNNY DIDN'T HESITATE TO ACCEPT Tate's offer of a calming donut at a nearby bakery. The short walk to the shop was chilly, but she certainly didn't mind.

She sat at a small table next to the window and warmed her hands while Tate ordered donuts and coffee. Bunny asked for decaf; she'd had enough excitement for one day. She didn't need any stimulants, thank you very much.

Trying not to stare, she stole peeks at him while he stood at the counter. She'd never considered herself a beard woman, but she found his very seductive. Dark and trimmed close, peppered with silver flecks, it emphasized the strength of his jaw line. When he smiled at the cashier, lines appeared around his eyes. Nice lines. Lines she could imagine caressing with her finger, then kissing lightly as she made her way down...to those full lips.

"One small decaf," Tate said, shaking Bunny back to earth. "And a glazed donut."

"Thank you," she said.

After placing their order on the table, Tate laid the brown tray on top of the stack behind him. He sat, scooted in, looked at Bunny and smiled, but said nothing.

Bunny panicked. What should she say? She was horrible at small talk. She had hated the many required business dinner parties when she was married to Richard for that very reason. She considered talking about the weather, but they'd talked about the cold and sunny day on the walk over. It had been appropriate then.

"Um, thank you again. For helping at the Pines." She shook her head. "I don't carry much clout there, I'm afraid."

"What's that all about?" Tate bit into his donut, then quickly wiped away bits of glaze at the edges of his mouth. He licked his lips to catch anything there, and she went warm all over just watching.

"Um, you mean, the business with the key?"

"Yeah."

"I'm not really sure. My sister seems to have taken control. She has power of attorney or something."

"That doesn't seem very smart. What if something happened to her?"

"She's probably invincible. I'm not entirely sure she's actually human. She might be a cyborg."

Tate laughed, which put Bunny more at ease. "Wait," she said suddenly. "Why were you at the Pines?"

"Checking on a condo my dad bought. He decided to keep his house instead, so we're trying to sell it." Tate stared at his cup, and Bunny wondered if he did so because he was uncomfortable.

"Why?"

"Why what?"

"Why did he decide to keep his house if he went to the trouble of buying a condo?"

He shrugged. "He's..." He wasn't used to confiding in people. "He's not well." Tate cleared his throat. "He's been given six months at the most."

She placed her hand on his, an instant reaction to such horrible news. His hand was warm and rough. "I'm sorry. That's terrible."

"Thanks. Thanks." He squeezed her hand lightly, and a little tingle ran up her arm. "We've hired a company that provides nursing care, and as his time grows closer, hospice will take over. He's very comfortable right now."

She pulled her hand away and cupped her coffee with both hands, sipping gently. "It has to be very hard on you and your daughter. Do you have other family helping?"

"My sister is in D.C."

"That's good. I can't believe you took on the school play with this going on. That has to be a lot of work. And dealing with something like this." She shook her head. "I don't know how you do it. I'd be a mess."

"You're probably closer to your father than I am to mine."

Bunny was surprised at the coolness with which Tate laid that one out on the table. "Oh."

"And I'm very jealous that your father plays *Steel Warriors*. He's very hip and happening, I gotta say."

She shook her head and laughed. But she still felt sad, deep down, about his earlier comment. "I wonder if my sister knows about his addiction. Do you think I should be concerned?"

"I think it gives him something to do. Did you see those guys? They were passed out like a bunch of teens who'd had themselves a really fun night."

He had a point. Maybe Bunny should let sleeping old men play. An awkward silence settled between them. Bunny wondered what else to say. She had plenty of questions.

Are you married? He had a child, but didn't wear a wedding ring. She didn't know how to ask that without coming across as forward.

Are you hot for Hildie Page? Again, not something you just blurt out.

Did angels sprinkle moon dust in your hair? Well now, that's just plain silly, Bunny. You can't ask that. Of course they did.

Tate broke the lull. "I wonder if the kids are done running those lines?"

Bunny wrinkled forehead. "What?"

"Charlie and Willow. They're running lines with some other kids from the cast."

"At the Java Hut?"

"Yeah. You didn't know?"

"I guess I'm lucky he told me he was going there. He just said he was meeting friends. He's not a real talker." Sort of like you, she thought to herself. Although that was hardly fair. A donut shop was hardly a place to have deep conversations.

"Most teenage boys aren't, so I'd say he's pretty normal." Tate smiled at Bunny, and the lines around his eyes made her melt inside.

"Yeah." For a split second, Bunny considered doing something wild and crazy. Something she'd never done in her life—ask a man out on a date. As soon as she thought of the idea, she had a million reasons why it was crazy and far-fetched, not the least of which was that they worked together. Dating could make for awkward moments on the job if it didn't go well or if he laughed in her face after she did the asking.

Tate looked at his watch. "I uh…"

"Oh," interrupted Bunny, taking the cue to get moving. "I'm sure you have things to and so do I. Tomorrow is another work week and all." What did that mean? She wanted to slap herself when she said stupid things. She stood. "Thank you for this. You've been great today."

"What's an old high school buddy for, anyway?"

She raised an eyebrow. They'd hardly been buddies, but she wished they had been. The sentiment was nice, though. She'd take it.

Walking to the door, she panicked that they'd have nothing to say on the way back to Whispering Pines. She decided to feign a need to stop in at the drugstore for some items and told him to go on without her. "See you tomorrow," she said.

He waved, and she watched his back as he walked away. With one hand on the door to the drugstore, she thought about what Barb had told her. Had Tate asked Colt about her because he was interested?

The man was hard to read. She'd certainly had men interested in her before, and usually they were very obvious. With each step he took, his hands in his pocket, staring at the sidewalk beneath his feet, she hoped. Hoped he would look back at her. If he did, she thought, that would be the sign.

The farther he walked, the further her optimism plummeted. She pulled on the door. Heck, she thought. Might as well pick up some shampoo while I'm here.

Then, just as she stepped through the doorway, she checked one more time and caught him looking over his shoulder at her.

CHAPTER SIXTEEN

ATE DECIDED ENTERING THE NATURE Center from the front was far more interesting than slipping in through the back door. In fact, he'd arrived a few minutes after nine for several mornings in a row now. With each passing day, he noticed that he wasn't the only one who seemed happier around the place.

On Thursday, Crabby Abby actually smiled at him. Her hair looked different—not so wild—and he wondered if a different hair style could actually put someone in a better mood.

And this morning, after wondering why Bunny wasn't at the reception desk, he heard voices in the conference room. He went to see if he'd forgotten a meeting. When he poked his nose in, Bunny turned and smiled. One of her hands hovered over Olga's face.

"Am I interrupting something?" he asked.

"I'm giving Olga some pointers," Bunny said.

Tate recognized the items laid out on the long, wide table: makeup. He suppressed a snicker.

Olga's head was tipped backwards. One eye was closed, and the other attempted to focus on Tate. "She give me lesson on making face pretty. Thees face can use all the help it can get."

"Stop that," Bunny told her. "You have a very pretty face. You just hide it with those glasses. You should get contact lenses."

"We see how you do with the mascara and blushes. Then we talk contacts lenses."

"I'll, uh, leave you two to whatever it is you're doing. I won't tell Abigail you're in here."

"It her idea!" Olga shouted. "Bunny do her hair, make big change for Abigail. She got hot date this weekend with George. But shh—that is secret." She sat forward and shot Tate a wink.

Tate hoped the wink wasn't a hint for him to ask Olga out.

Bunny shrugged at Tate. "I'm almost done," she told him. "Olga, sit back. Let me finish."

"Okie dokie." Olga obeyed and Tate stepped back to leave.

"Tate!" Bunny called out, stopping him. "A man called for you last night after you left. He said it was important, but wouldn't leave a message and said he didn't need your voicemail. He did ask when you'd be in today."

"He didn't say what it was about?"

She shook her head. "Sorry."

"Thanks. I guess if it's important enough, he'll call back."

"He said he'd stop by."

That was a little strange. He wasn't in the middle of any important projects, and most people he did business with left messages. He wondered if it was personal in nature. Or maybe it was one of the dads he was working with on the set for *Kiss Me, Kate*. "Okay. Thanks."

He closed the door and let Bunny finish performing miracles on Olga.

The rest of the day was ordinary. Tate met with his staff about pre-school and elementary school programs, bluebird nest box monitoring, and the upcoming spring stream cleanup effort.

He then drove to the north side of town to meet with the arborists about some diseased trees bordering the nature paths. He offered them his view of what should be done. Ultimately, it was the arborists' decision, but the town always consulted with him, since the natural makeup of Rustic Woods was what made Rustic Woods the model for nature-oriented planned communities around the country.

By five, when he should have been going home, he still had emails to go through. If he didn't, more would just pile on over the weekend.

He handled several quickly, deleted a few spam emails, and was reading another when his phone buzzed from up front. "Tate?"

He talked into the intercom. "You're still here, Bunny? You should go home. I'll lock up."

"There's someone here to see you," Bunny said.

"Who is it?"

"He says he's your brother."

Tate froze. He stared at the phone's orange intercom light.

"Tate?" Bunny asked.

"Yeah. Yeah." He wiped his palms on his jeans. "Uh, tell him I'll...I'll be right there."

He stood. He sat. He stood. He closed his email and powered down his computer. After a minute, staring at the blank screen, he pulled open his top drawer, grabbed his keys and wallet, walked slowly out of his office, and headed directly away from the reception area.

For the first time all week, he left out the back door.

At home, Tate sat at his kitchen table pulling swigs from a long neck beer and reading the note Willow had left. *Tater Pop—running lines at Nina's house, then going for Pizza with some of cast after. Text if not okay. Be home by 9, promise. XXOO*

He had to re-read it several times because his mind kept shifting to images of Samuel being that close to him, and his own inability to face the man he'd contacted first. He slammed the bottle on the table, angry at himself. He was a coward. But he was angry at Samuel, too. He'd left a message with his cell phone number, yet the man had sought out his place of employment and chosen to show up unannounced. Tate wondered if Samuel was playing some kind of game. He was probably visit Morton next or maybe he'd already tried that.

Thank goodness Tate had finally talked May into spending time with Mort. She'd picked him up the night before and they were traveling to Charlotte, North Carolina so Mort could visit their mother's grave. Morton had complained often over the years that his wife, Alice, chose to be buried near her parents in Charlotte. Tate never understood her choice either, how could he? She'd died when he was an infant. Hard to understand someone he'd never known didn't know. And that went for his brother, as well.

Hating to sit and dwell, Tate decided that a shower might make him feel better. He was in his room pulling his t-shirt over his head when the doorbell rang.

It was either a drive-by tree guy wanting to give Tate an estimate to take down the big oak that leaned over the house, or it was Samuel. If Samuel had figured out where he worked, he probably had figured out where he lived.

Tate yanked the t-shirt back down over his chest and walked from his room. What most people didn't know when they stood at his front door, was that a thin glass window in the hallway from the kitchen to his bedroom offered a perfect view of the visitor's back. If it was Samuel, he could decide whether or not to answer. If it was a tree guy, he'd take that shower and forget the door.

With his head against the wall, he peeked through the pane. If that was a tree guy, he had a great ass.

Tate stepped away from the wall. A smile tugged at one corner of his mouth.

The doorbell rang again. He hesitated, torn between the need for solitude and the desire for company. Okay, not just any company. Bunny Bergen.

She had a way of making him want to talk about himself. He hadn't met anyone with that effect on him in years.

The third ring made his decision for him. Evidently she wasn't giving up easily.

Tate padded, barefoot, to the door and opened it. He couldn't think of any sensible words to greet her. What did she know? Did Samuel tell her anything? Everything?

She held up an envelope. "He left this for you."

Tate didn't take it. Couldn't take it. He looked into her green eyes and found comfort, but still, he didn't say anything.

"Do you want to talk?" she asked, taking a step closer.

He shrugged. "It's a long story. Silly plot. Not a lot of action."

She pulled his hand from its grip on the door, pressed the envelope into his palm, then closed her own fingers around his and squeezed. Her hands were soft and offered the same comfort as her eyes. "I have time."

There was no way he could say no to her. He opened the door wider. "Want a beer?"

She stepped in, giving a quick glance around the interior. "Sure." She smiled at him. "Charlie and Willow are at Nina's house. They're going for pizza after." She closed the door behind her.

Tate nodded, and hated that his hands were shaking. "Come on in," he said. "The kitchen is back here." He pointed the way, motioning for Bunny to precede him down the hallway. Mostly he was being a gentlemen, but he also wanted to take in her scent as she passed.

He folded the envelope and stuffed it into his pocket.

Bunny stood, looking a little awkward in the middle of his kitchen. "You have a nice house."

He pulled a chair out from the table. "Have a seat." He opened the fridge and pulled out another long neck. His remained unfinished on the counter. "Thanks," he continued. "The Nature Center provides decent living quarters, and Willow gives it the feminine touch it needs. The walls would be bare if she weren't around."

Bunny nodded and sat, smiling. "Where does her mother live?"

There it was. The question he always avoided. The inevitable question that never got easier to answer, no matter how many years ticked away.

He had, however, grown used to spitting the answer out bluntly. Made the transition to the sorrowful and sympathetic reaction quicker and less painful. "She passed away when Willow was three."

Everyone asked how, so he'd learned to put it all out there. "Riding a bike—a truck plowed into her. They say she died instantly and probably didn't feel any pain." He took a long pull on his beer while handing Bunny hers, and then sat down himself.

He usually avoided eye contact when he gave his spiel, but not this time. He held Bunny's gaze. Her eyes were wide, and he knew what she was thinking. "Don't feel bad. You didn't know. I try to keep my personal life private." He sat across from her, beer in front of him, hands encircling the bottle as if it might run away if he let go.

She nodded. "I understand." She allowed a whisper of a smile to show. "Sometimes I wish my life were more private." She shrugged. "A lot of times. What was her name?"

"Jill."

"Do you have a picture?"

Most people didn't ask to see a picture. They usually tried to change the subject or ask how Willow dealt with growing up without having a mother. "Uh, yeah."

He stood and walked to the living room, noticing, for the first time, the cold tile on his bare feet. In fact, the entire house was chilled. He'd turn the heat up in a minute.

He unhooked a frame from the wall and returned, handing it to Bunny. The picture was one he had taken of Jill and Willow at Yosemite National Park. Willow was two and a half at the time. They had lived in California, and Tate and Jill worked long days, earning great money in their white collar computer jobs. That trip was the first they'd taken in over a year.

"She was beautiful." Bunny's smile was genuine. "Willow looks just like her."

Tate scooted his chair closer, really looking at the photo for the first time in years. Before he knew it, he was telling Bunny about how he met Jill during his senior year in college. How he had followed her to San Jose, purposely taking a job in the same company. How he had proposed to her during a weekend getaway to San Francisco, kneeling as he clung to a bar on a trolley car and how the passengers had applauded when she said yes. How they agreed to name their daughter after Jill's favorite tree and had planned to name their next child River if it was a girl, and Tristan if it was a boy. How her sudden death made him question what he was doing with his life.

They'd had such a short time together, doing jobs that were unfulfilling. So with Willow still a toddler, he quit his job, spent time with his daughter, and reconsidered his choices. Eventually, he went back to school and trained in something more fulfilling and enriching that allowed him more flexibility as a single parent. He chose wildlife biology, knowing he wanted a career as a naturalist.

He'd spoken nearly non-stop for twenty minutes. Bunny had asked questions here and there, but overall, he did the talking, and she did the listening.

By the end of his story, he realized that his chair was touching hers and that he had his arm wrapped around the back of it, leaning the slightest bit against her shoulders. He hadn't spilled that much of himself to anyone since Jill's death. Not even May. The woman next to him was so open and genuine and kind that he felt almost completely at ease baring his soul to her.

Bunny placed the framed photo on the table with gentle care. "You were lucky to have each other," she said.

He was surprised by the depth of her statement. He'd heard little more than well-meaning, empty platitudes over the years: *I'm so sorry, for your loss* and *She'll always be alive in your heart*. But he couldn't recall anyone ever saying *You were lucky to have each other*. Yes, he thought, they were. For the first time in fifteen years, he felt free of the burden of her memory. Not the burden of having loved her, but of the memory of that love. For the first time, someone else touched him deeply and profoundly. Someone he desired to kiss not just for the pleasure of it, but because every cell in his body yearned for her, every synapse in his brain fired a passion for her.

"Bunny, I..."

At the sound of her name, she looked up, their faces just inches apart.

He studied the gold flecks against the green in her eyes, followed the slim contour of her nose, the sweet curves of her lips. "I..."

He felt warmth through his beard as she wrapped her hands around his face. And then there was the soft, heavenly taste of her lips on his.

CHAPTER SEVENTEEN

ATE'S MOUTH PRESSED BUNNY'S LIGHTLY at first. Gently. She pulled his face closer to hers and parted her lips to accept his increasingly passionate exploration. His tongue tasted like beer. Feeling a tickle, she giggled.

He pulled away, but kept his hand cradling the back of her head.

"What?" He breathed heavily.

"I've never kissed a man with a beard before. It tickles."

He smiled. "Is that okay?"

Her own breathing was out of control. "It's very okay."

His molten eyes grew more intent and he leaned back in, kissing her bottom lip and sliding his tongue across and in.

She moaned with pleasure and ran a hand down his shoulder and gripped his bicep.

In response, he ran a hand behind her back and pulled her to him. Awkward in the chairs and consumed by the moment, she flung her leg over him, straddling him in his chair.

They kissed long and hard and deep, her fingers caressing his hair, his hardness pressing against her.

Sweet mother of madness he was good. She ran a hand under his t-shirt and up his chest, stopping to enjoy the thrill of his hand on her thigh.

Finally, when the intensity seemed nearly unbearable, he pulled his face from her just enough to whisper. Their noses were still touching. "Not here," he said quietly.

Then giving her lips another gentle kiss, he eased her off of him.

They stood, pressed against each other, and Bunny felt like they were dancing again as they had so many years ago. Only this time, her dream would be fulfilled. He took her hand as she stared into those deep, endlessly dark eyes, and willingly followed him to his bed.

Afterward, they lay entwined under the sheet and a blanket. The air was chilled, but Tate's body kept her warm. They faced each other, his leg curled over both of hers, his arm around her, and his hand pressed pleasantly against the small of her back.

She ran her hand along his upper arm. She loved the feel of it. The sky had turned dark since she arrived, and she thought about Charlie and Willow. "What time is it?" she asked.

Tate propped himself on one elbow and squinted over her shoulder, giving it a kiss when he leaned back. "Eight forty-five." He groaned. "Willow said she'd be home by nine."

Bunny bolted upright. "We need to dress." She rolled over, a bit panicked at the thought of being caught in Tate's bed by his teenage daughter, but also frustrated that they couldn't spend more time together.

He'd been just as she imagined. Gentle, but passionate. And he knew his way around her parts better than any man she'd ever been with.

She slipped on her underwear while Tate did the same. As she zipped up her skirt, Tate zipped up his jeans. "We, um, never did talk about that man and the envelope," she said hesitantly, not wanting to upset the moment. But it had been the reason she'd come here.

"It's another long story," he said, thrusting an arm through one sleeve of his t-shirt.

"You have a lot of those?"

"Let's just say that dysfunction runs rampant in my family."

She buttoned her blouse and shrugged. "I don't believe there are any dysfunctional families. Everyone I've ever met claims they're from a dysfunctional family, so that means wacky is normal."

"Wacky?"

Tate's smile made her tingle all over. As if he meant to tingle her some more, he strode over and pulled her in for a long, deep, toe-curling kiss.

"I need to get my shoes on before your daughter gets home, and you're avoiding the subject."

"He's my brother, Samuel. I haven't seen him in a few years, give or take a couple of decades."

Bunny had just slipped her foot into her other shoe when they both saw the light from a car's headlights pass the bedroom window. Outside, a car's engine rumbled as it pulled into the driveway.

"Oh no!" Bunny said, looking to Tate for guidance. Would he want her to sneak out a back door?

He laughed and took her hand, pulling her to the kitchen. "It's fine, our beers are still on the table. Act natural."

Bunny lacked confidence that she could act anywhere near natural. She'd just made love to, literally, the man of her dreams. The mere touch of his hand on hers caused every nerve to scream *Hallelujah!*

Act natural? She didn't think so. She stopped, tugging on his hand. "I'm going to just leave, and if I pass her, I'll just say I was dropping something off."

"Yeah. Okay," he agreed. "That works." He kissed her one more time, holding the back of her head with his hand. Then she walked quickly to the front door, looking back at him.

"I'll, uh…"

She heard the hesitation his voice.

"It's okay," she said waving off his stutter. "This doesn't have to mean anything." *Actually, it does. It needs to be so much more. Please call me tomorrow.* "You don't have to call me. Or anything." She put her hand on the doorknob and turned. "I hope you work things out with your brother."

When she pulled on the door, Willow was there reaching to let herself in. Her eyes widened, and Bunny wasn't sure if she was startled at the door opening or at the person who opened it. "Hi, Willow!" she said as naturally as she could manage.

"Hi," Willow replied, a backpack slung over one shoulder. She gave Bunny a sideways glance and shot Tate a what's-going-on-here look.

"I just dropped something off for your dad. Work-related stuff." Willow nodded. "Cool."

Feeling the need to escape an uncomfortable scene, Bunny threw a little wave to Tate. "See you Monday. Bye, Willow."

"Bye," said Willow.

Tate, cool as a cucumber, gave Bunny a light nod. "Monday."

In her car, she calmly backed out of the driveway and drove a few yards before pulling to the side of the road and slamming the gear shift into park.

Her mind was on fire, and her stomach churned. Overwhelmed, she finally let go, put her face in her hands and bawled, her body wracked by heaving sobs.

CHAPTER EIGHTEEN

WILLOW WAS PARTICULARLY CHATTY ABOUT her evening and insisted Tate sit with her over cookies and milk while she told him all about the funny things that happened at Nina's house. How Charlie made sure he sat next to Willow in the booth at Full Moon Pizza and how Nina looked irritated when he did so.

"I think she likes him," Willow said, dipping a chocolate chip cookie into her glass. "But she's kind of weird about it. She was really quiet on the drive home."

Tate tried to stay focused on the conversation. Although it wasn't so much a conversation as a monologue. He smiled and nodded, but intermittently his mind drifted to Bunny or sometimes to Samuel. What a day.

"The more I get to know him," Willow continued on some train of thought that he'd partially missed, "the more I realize how really nice he is. He's kind of quiet, but really nice."

Okay, thought Tate, she'd mentioned Charlie before so she must be talking about him now. He took an educated guess and entered an observation. "His mom is nice, so that doesn't surprise me."

Willow narrowed his eyes at him. "You didn't tell her that I liked him did you?"

"Of course not." He stole the cookie from her hand and took a bite. "We work together. It's not like we're..." *lovers*. "I mean, we're associates."

He hadn't pulled the wool over Willow's eyes, and he knew it. She snuck a glance toward his bedroom.

His bedside light was still on.

She looked back at Tate. "Uh-huh." She took another cookie from the jar and bit into it, not taking her eyes off Tate.

He stood to avoid her stare, emptied the two bottles of beer into the sink, and turned the faucet on to rinse. He needed to change the subject. "I saw on the calendar that the quarter is almost over. Are you keeping your grades up with all of this rehearsing you're doing?"

"You asked me that yesterday."

"Did you answer me?"

"Uh-huh."

Damn. She was right. He remembered now.

He stretched his arms and forced a yawn. "I'm going to go read in my room and then hit the sack." He tousled her hair, still avoiding eye contact, and padded down the hall.

"Dad." His daughter's voice stopped him.

He didn't look back. "She *is* really nice. Charlie talks about her a lot. In a good way. Not a lot of kids think enough of their parents to talk about them."

He turned and smiled. He wanted to cry. "Thanks. Lock the door and turn out the lights when you go to bed?"

"Sure, Tater Pop."

Tate was the type to fall asleep the minute his head hit the pillow. Tonight he tossed and turned for thirty minutes or more. When he finally dozed off, he dreamed Bunny was at her reception desk wearing glasses and aiming a laser pointer at a white board to indicate categories of proper beauty care. Olga and Abigail scribbled note on steno pads. The phone rang, but Bunny wouldn't answer it. The thing just rang and rang and rang.

Eventually, he realized in the dream that the phone was his real phone and that he needed to wake up and answer the damn thing.

He threw back the covers and scrambled groggily to the kitchen where their only landline telephone hung on the wall.

By the time he was halfway down the hallway, he heard Willow pick up. "Hello?" her voice sounded as tired as he felt. "Is everything okay?" she asked, suddenly sounding more awake and concerned.

Tate rounded the corner where Willow held out the phone for him. "It's Aunt May. Morty's in the hospital."

They made the six and a half hour drive bolstered by hourly doses of coffee and listening to Tate's Eagles CDs. He was lucky Willow liked them as much as he did.

They sang out loud to "Hotel California," and Willow played the air guitar to Don Felder's riff. He would have taken Joe Walsh's role if he hadn't been responsible for keeping the car on road.

They watched the dark sky turn a stunning shade of pink to "Tequila Sunrise."

Willow said she didn't really get the appeal of "Desperado," but that the other songs more than made up for it.

For Tate, "Victim of Love" rang particularly true in the moment, but it was "Do Something," which played somewhere around Greensboro, that caused him to go quiet and think.

He decided to make a confession. "I've told you about Uncle Samuel, right?" he asked Willow.

"Yeah. Not much. Aunt May called him a Rat Bastard once when she was a little tipsy."

Tate flicked an eyebrow. The name fit, he guessed. "He showed up at the Center yesterday."

Her eyes widened, and she turned in her seat to face him. "Out of the blue?"

"Not exactly."

"Have you been talking to him? What's he like?"

He shook his head. "A few weeks ago I hired an investigator to locate him. They gave me a phone number and an address."

"Where does he live now?"

"Seattle."

"Boy, he did get about as far away as he could get, didn't he?"

"I left a message on his phone last week."

"You told him about Morty?"

"More or less."

"Have you talked at all?"

Tate shook his head. "When he showed up at the Nature Center..."

"Oh my God. You chickened out, didn't you?"

"Can you not be so good at predicting my actions, please?"

"This already happened, so I didn't predict it. I made an educated guess that you acted like a chicken. So you snuck out? Seriously? Where's your cell phone?"

She didn't bother to wait for an answer. Instead she reached over and patted his shirt pocket. She shook her head some more and pulled it out, lighting the display. "Six missed calls all from the same number...when did he show up, five o'clock?" She flipped and scrolled. "You shut your ringer off?"

"I haven't seen the man since I was six years old. He hates our father."

"Morty isn't an easy man to like. You can't exactly hold that against him."

Tate worked the envelope from his jeans pocket while trying to keep his eyes and car on the road. Eventually, he was able to wriggle it free from where it had remained, unopened, since Bunny handed it to him the night before.

He gave it to Willow.

"What's this?" she asked.

He checked his side mirror while turning his indicator on so he could pass the slow car ahead of him. "I haven't read it yet."

"You want me to?"

"Read it to me."

"Why can't you..."

"He knew Morton was an asshole, and he still left. I was alone." He tightened his grip on the steering wheel.

"You had a sister."

"I wanted a brother."

Willow pressed Tate's arm, and he felt ashamed of his weakness. He was weak for not finishing what he had started and weak for leaning on his daughter.

He shook his head and tried to retrieve the envelope. "Don't. Don't read it. I'm sorry."

Willow yanked her arm out of his reach. "No. We'll do this." She squeezed his arm again.

Tate watched the road. *We'll do this.* She sounded like her mother just then.

Willow unsealed the envelope and unfolded the recognizable Rustic Woods Nature Center letterhead. Bunny must have given him the paper.

"Tate," Willow read, "I don't like phones. I'm staying at The Monument, room seven-twelve. Samuel." She lifted an eyebrow. "Wow. The Monument. That's an expensive hotel, isn't it?"

"Understatement."

"What does he do—do you know?"

"CEO. Western Skies Airlines."

"Holy Crap. Really? That's kind of high profile. You could've just asked me to do a Google search, and I would've charged you a lot less."

"He changed his last name."

"Oh." She folded the paper, returning it to the envelope. "To what?"

"Alice. Samuel Alice."

"Your mother's name."

Tate squinted to read the freeway signs above him. "Yup."

They arrived at St. Vincent's Hospital tired and hungry and especially not ready for May's dramatics.

"What took you so long?" she demanded, rising from a purple chair in the hospital lounge. She hugged Tate briskly. "It's been hell here. I am not cut out for this. I'm just not."

"Calm down. It's a six and a half hour drive, and we had to take time to pack a few things. We got here as quickly as we could."

She pointed to him. "This is your fault."

"That's crazy."

"I didn't want to do this."

Tate's shoulders cramped with tension. None of them wanted to do this. He tried to keep his voice even. "You didn't tell me that."

"What was I supposed to say? 'No, I don't want to drive our father to see his dead wife's grave before he dies?'"

He rubbed the back of his neck. "Where is he?"

"Third floor."

"Have you talked to the doctor recently?"

"The doctor?" His sister threw her arms in the air with a predictable amount of drama. "As in just one? Try again. There's a new coat talking to me every time I go up there."

They rode the elevator to the third floor in silence, staring at the lights above the door as they marked their progress.

As the door opened, May put her arm around Willow. "How's the play coming?"

"Good," Willow nodded.

"Charlie—how that's going?" she asked as they filed out.

"Really good," Willow said, grinning.

Tate allowed himself a smile, but stayed focused on finding Morton's room. "Which way, May?"

His sister pointed down the corridor to their left. "Room three-twelve."

"You coming?"

"I've had enough of him. You deal with it for a while."

Tate rolled his eyes. That had been her mantra since he'd moved back last summer.

"I'll be over there," she indicated a small alcove of chairs and vending machines. "Wanna sit with me, Willow?"

Willow looked at Tate, hopeful. "Is that okay?"

He nodded. May had warned them on the phone that Morton was crankier than usual.

He turned toward Morton's room, but stopped. Taking his cell phone from his shirt pocket, he handed it to Willow. "Answer that if it rings." He looked her straight in the eyes, hoping she'd translate his meaning. *Answer if Samuel calls.*

She held his gaze, and he knew she understood.

"Got it," she said.

Tate found room three-twelve, but he stood outside the room a moment, taking a deep breath and preparing himself before entering.

Mort was awake. Drained, pale. Looking years older, but awake. Tubes and wires monitored him and fed him fluids and oxygen.

"Hey, Mort," said Tate. "Couldn't wait til you got home, huh?"

CHAPTER NINETEEN

UNNY SAT AT HER DINING room table, hovered over a cup of coffee, pen in hand, scribbling a list of things she needed to get done over the weekend. The more things she gave herself to do, she figured, the less she'd think about Tate.

Number one on her list: call Peggy Rubenstein. According to Barb, Peggy had updated her real estate license and was looking for new clients. Peggy seemed to know everyone in Rustic Woods, so Bunny imagined she wouldn't have trouble getting started again. She loved Peggy, so even though she dreaded selling her home, at least she'd be working with someone who could put her at ease during the trauma.

She also had groceries to buy. Charlie and Michael seemed to empty the cupboards faster than she could fill them. Call Michael—another item.

He had gone to Richard's again for the weekend, but he had forgotten his soccer uniform, and he had a Sunday game. She wanted to arrange to get it to him.

She stared at the list. Not long enough. She pulled the coffee mug to her lips and sipped. Thoughts of Tate nuzzling and kissing her neck floated into her mind. Her eyes closed, feeling again the warmth of his breath near her ear as he whispered *don't move* when moving became inevitable, inescapable. She needed to...

Oh, noodles! She forced her eyes to the list again. Think, think, what else did she need to do?

Her mind wandered again. The firmness of his arms under her hands as she grasped him when...

She slammed the pen down, pushed herself from her chair, and stomped to the kitchen faucet. She turned the cold water on and splashed her face with it. Well, that worked on her face, but it didn't really do the job. She needed a cold shower.

She filled a glass with water and was beginning to gulp when her cell phone rang.

Running back to the dining room, she fumbled with the thing before focusing on the display to see who was calling. She didn't recognize the number. "Hello?" she said warily.

"Ms. Bergen?"

"Who is this?"

"Nancy Mills. From Whispering Pines."

"Oh." Bunny was caught off-guard. She never received calls from Whispering Pines. Her heart nearly leapt out of her throat. "Is everything okay? Is it Daddy?"

"I'm not calling from the office. Your father is healthy as far as I know, but I am calling about him. I thought you should know some things."

"Nancy, you're worrying me."

"No, no. Don't worry. But please promise me you won't tell anyone about this call. I'd get fired in a split second. I'm looking for another job, but until then..."

"You have my word. What's going on?"

"Your sister learned about the video game parties and has removed them from his unit. She's interviewing addiction treatment centers."

"You have got to be kidding me."

"He's very upset. She had a nurse in to sedate him yesterday before taking him to her house."

"Oh my God. Doesn't he have any rights?"

"He signed over medical power of attorney."

"But he's in his right mind. He knows what he's doing."

"She claims he isn't. Anyway, that's really about all I know. About that, anyway. She donates a ton of money for building improvements and senior activities, and now she's on the Board of Directors."

"When did that happen?"

"A few months ago. She does what she wants, basically. Mr. Baker is afraid of her."

Bunny closed her eyes, and released a heavy sigh. "Thank you for letting me know. I appreciate it."

"I couldn't let it go, Ms. Bergen. He was so upset. He kept saying that she'd stolen all of his phones and was begging someone to call you."

"Thank you again. I promise to keep your name out of this."

She clicked the phone off. Well, if she needed something to throw cold water on her libido, that had done the job.

While showering, Bunny considered her options. Hiring a lawyer to fight Demon's claim seemed logical, but completely out of her financial reach. Her father could afford the fight, but Demon had control of his money, too.

Trying to convince Demon to rethink the addiction treatment idea—forget it. Demon did what Demon wanted to do, and common sense never entered the picture. She craved control and did whatever necessary to keep a stranglehold. Bunny wished someone would declare her mentally unfit.

Barb knew a guy who'd once had mafia connections. Maybe he could make a phone call. Demon weighed about a thousand pounds. The sharks would be in feast heaven. Bunny smiled at the image, then gave herself a mental slap on the hand. The last thought was unkind, and she had recently dedicated herself to pure and benevolent reflection. Referring to her sister as Demon, however, was exempt.

In the kitchen, she moved the few dirty dishes in the sink to the dishwasher and checked the activities calendar on the fridge for Michael's Sunday soccer game time.

Realizing that the month was now March gave her a brilliant idea. Demon's birthday was March 19th. Bunny rarely did anything special for her sister's birthday, but in an attempt to keep the peace, she would usually call her on that day. What Bunny really needed was to see her father in person—to find out just how upset he was.

Showing up to surprise Demon with an early birthday present—that could work. Demon was rarely suspicious when people were nice to her since she expected everyone to adore and worship her anyway.

Bunny smiled at her own genius.

Bunny arrived on the doorstep of Demon's palatial estate with a gift bag dangling from one hand and her purse thrown over the other shoulder.

The Christmas before last, Demon had given Bunny the most horrific smelling perfume she'd ever encountered. It was called Chasm, and she joked with her boys that it they should have called it Spasm since that's what happened when you got near the stink of it.

Bunny had decided to repay the gesture by purchasing the cheapest, rosiest scented crap she could find at the drugstore. She spent more money on the gift bag than she did the bottle of cheap perfume.

Rolling her shoulders to release the tension pinching them like a vise, Bunny breathed deeply and pushed the doorbell.

Lovely chimes echoed loudly enough to be heard through the door. *Ding-dong, bong-bong, bong-dong, ding-ding.*

A Spanish woman holding a feather duster opened the door. Bunny peeked around her. "Um, is Ms. Hobbs here? I'm her sister."

"Bunny? Bunny?" Her father's voice echoed through the grand, marble floored foyer, but she didn't see him. "Is that you?"

Throwing manners aside, Bunny pushed past the feather duster woman. "Daddy?"

"What's going on here?" Demon's voice rang out from the left, and the sound of heels clicking on the marble drew nearer as Bunny and her father embraced.

Seeing Bunny, Demon's face crumpled immediately into a frown, but then relaxed into a broad but thin-lipped smile.

Bunny thought she looked like she'd just relieved herself of a painful bowel movement. Of course, Bunny thought, the woman *was* a painful bowel movement. Forget peaceful reflection. Impossible where her sister was concerned. Impossible.

Bunny decided to play it as cool and oblivious as possible, although it was hard with Daddy digging his nails into her arm.

"Deena!" She lifted the gift bag for show. "Happy Birthday! A few days early."

Demon clacked closer, her feet overflowing the shiny black shoes she always wore. She smiled, but with a noticeable wary tilt to her head. She accepted the bag while Bunny cringed inwardly at the amount of makeup her sister managed to cake onto her flabby face. "More than a few days, I would say, but thank you. Deena always loves her birthday goodies."

That was another habit that always annoyed Bunny; Deena frequently referred to herself in the third person.

"Such a nice surprise. I'd ask you to stay for tea, but—"

"So Daddy," Bunny asked, stepping right over Demon's attempt to escape scrutiny. "You're visiting Deena for the weekend?"

He shook his head vehemently. "They're counting on me. I want to go back home."

"Who's counting—"

"He hasn't been feeling—"

"Daddy who's counting on you?" Bunny spit out before Demon could interrupt again.

"The boys. The battle begins at five tonight."

"Do you hear this crazy talk?" Deena said. "I'm taking him—"

"It's not crazy talk! It's my hobby, and I have a good time. Let me have a good time, dammit!" He stomped his foot. "You know who needs to see a damn doctor? You!" He bugged his eyes out at Demon, and Bunny suppressed a hearty laugh. "Get your stomach stapled or something, for crying out loud. You're gonna keel over from a heart attack long before I die from playing video games. Addiction, my ass!"

Before Bunny knew what was happening, Daddy was pulling her to the door. "Quick!" he yelled. "Get me out of this hell hole! She had me watching some British crap on TV last night—rich people and their servants. I don't care if Mary can't have a baby or if Mr. Bates ever gets out of jail!"

He pulled her through the front door—not that she was exactly fighting him—and down the stone steps while Demon screamed behind them.

Luckily, her girth slowed her down, and Daddy was proving to be quite a sprinter.

He leaped into the passenger seat of Bunny's car with the grace of a puma and ordered Bunny to move it.

She fumbled with the keys, watching Deena stop to yell something to the Spanish feather duster lady in the house. Managing to get the key in the ignition and the car started, Bunny pulled the gear shift into reverse and screeched out of the driveway.

Her heart pounded, and her hands shook so violently she could barely keep the steering wheel steady.

"She'll call the police," she said, her voice cracking with nerves. "This is useless."

"Just drive! She doesn't have any control now that we're off her property."

Bunny's cell phone rang. "Daddy, can you grab that from my purse and see who it is?" Bunny figured it was Demon, but wanted to know anyway.

"Says it's Charlie. You want me to answer?"

"Yes, please."

"Yeah, Charlie—whaddya want? It's your grandfather. Your mother is driving. Yeah, I can give her a message—go ahead. Uh-huh. Uh-huh. What's the name again? Tate? Uh-huh. Okay. Hey, Charlie, don't hang up. Tell me, you ever play *Steel Warriors*?"

Bunny wanted to rip the phone from him and find out what Charlie had said about Tate. Her fingers white-knuckled the steering wheel. "Daddy..."

He kept talking into the phone to his grandson. "Some dudes and me are battling tonight at five. You have internet at your house? Okay. See you soon."

"Daddy, don't hang up—" She was too late. He'd ended the call. "What was that about?"

"We can't play at my place. Deena will spoil it. We'll have to move the game to your place."

"Tate—you said something about Tate."

"He had an emergency and wants you to call him on his cell phone. Charlie left the phone number on the kitchen table. Who is Tate, anyway? You got a new boyfriend?"

CHAPTER TWENTY

THE PHONE VIBRATED IN TATE'S hand, waking him from an uncomfortable snooze in an uncomfortable chair.

It took a moment before his eyes focused properly on the display. The area code was Northern Virginia. He answered groggily. "Yeah?"

"Tate, it's Bunny. Charlie gave me your number. Is this a good time?"

He rubbed his eyes and scanned the lounge. Willow sat across the room, staring at a television mounted in the corner. May was curled up, asleep, in a chair next to her. "Uh, yeah. Hang on a minute."

He covered the mouthpiece and whispered across the room "Willow!" She glanced back. "Going outside for a few."

She nodded and turned her attention back to whatever show she was watching.

"Hey, thanks for calling," Tate said, making his way out of the lounge and through the automatic doors at the front of the hospital. The sun was bright and warmed a long nook that was protected from the wind by walls. He was glad for the early spring here in North Carolina.

"Sure. What happened? Charlie said you're in North Carolina with your dad."

"Yeah. It's not good. My sister brought him down here. For a visit." He took a deep breath. "Anyway, he developed a high fever pretty quickly last night so she brought him to the ER, and he's having a lot of trouble."

"That's terrible. Are you doing okay?"

He leaned against the wall, letting the sun soothe his face. "Sure. Sure. Tired. We, uh, got the call about three a.m. and got on the road about four, I guess. I don't know, maybe five. But, uh, I was wondering if you could help me out." He asked the question, still wondering if there wasn't another way to handle this without involving the woman he'd just slept with. Hildie Page would have been the logical person to call, but he'd rather deal with Bunny Bergen any day of the week over horny Hildie.

"Absolutely," Bunny answered. "How?"

"I'm sure we're still going to be here tomorrow, but some of the kids from the crew are coming to my place to paint scenery..."

"Do you want me to call them?"

He squinted across the parking lot, noticing some trees beginning to bud. He closed his eyes and imagined Bunny's smile. He pictured the way her hair looked when she tucked it behind one ear and let it fall around her face. "Would you mind? I don't have their numbers with me—they're at home, but—and here's the real problem—I don't remember where I put the list. It could be in a couple of places."

"How do I get in?"

"I keep a key hidden around back under a stone Willow painted. It has flowers on it. Or butterflies maybe. Bright paint. You can't miss it. When you get in the house, call me, and I'll walk you through where to look."

"I can do that. I have a bit of a father issue going on myself right now—it might be a couple of hours."

"I shouldn't ask you to do this, then. You've got your own problems. I'll call Hildie." He didn't want to call Hildie, but he didn't want to burden Bunny, either. He was torn about how deeply he wanted her in his life. Last night had been good. Fantastic, if he was being honest with himself. But...

"Issue," she said. "I have an issue, not problem. I've got it handled."

He nodded and smiled at the confidence in her voice. "Thanks. And, uh...I guess I'll talk to you soon, then."

"Okay. And I'll start praying for your dad."

"That'd be great." Tate clicked off the phone. He didn't really believe prayer worked. Besides, if Morton had a soul, he needed more prayers than Bunny could offer.

His phone jingled, telling him a text had come in. He scrolled and clicked.

Landing in ten minutes. Tate closed his eyes again. He needed to prepare May.

"May, wake up." Tate shook her shoulder. "May." She'd fallen into a pretty deep sleep—a miracle considering how hard the cushions were in these chairs.

May opened her eyes and stretched her arms, then her legs. She spread her flowing floral skirt over her knees. She had removed her boots, and he noticed one of her purple socks had a small hole in the toe.

"Did something happen?" she asked, eyes still droopy. "New news?"

"I need to tell you something. Are you awake enough to talk?"

She sat up straight, eyes widening. "What happened?"

He put his hand on her knee. "Nothing. I just... remember we're in a public place, so don't scream or yell or flip out or—"

"One more 'or' and I'll rip your arm out of its socket, baby brother. I may look very peace and granola, but I'm tired and when I'm tired, I can be quite violent. Spit it out."

He sucked in a deep breath and tried to say the words he'd rehearsed, but they stuck in his throat. She was going to be so pissed. Maybe he should have taken her outside.

"Tate, what's going on?"

"Samuel's on his way from the airport," Willow said.

He snapped his head in her direction.

Willow shrugged. "Isn't that what you were—"

"What?" May's voice didn't sound angry. That was a good sign.

He tilted his head and waved a hand in Willow's general direction. "What she said."

May propped her elbows on her knees and buried her head in her hands. "I'm confused. You'd better give me a little more information. Like, before I faint. Or murder you."

"I had a guy find him for us."

"For you."

"Fine. For me. For him. For Morton."

"For Morton? Give me a break."

"Do you want the story or not?"

She made a grand gesture of allowing him to continue.

"I had a phone number, so I called him. Left a message—we didn't talk." He ran a hand through his hair and wished he could take a shower. And run away. Far away. "But yesterday he showed up at the Nature Center."

"Just like that."

"Pretty much."

"What'd he say—hey bro, how've you been doing the last thirty-four years? Sorry I've been out of touch?"

"I didn't talk to him."

"He snuck out the back door," Willow clarified.

May laughed.

Tate knew the laugh. It was her *Isn't-this-just-shitty?* laugh. She'd done a lot of that growing up with Morton for a father, trying to be some kind of a mother to Tate, and still attempting to live a normal teenage life of her own.

"I called him this morning after talking to the doctors. He's flying down and will be here soon. There." He smacked his palms on his thighs. "Any other questions, you can direct at him when he arrives."

He rose to go check on their father.

"Did you ever consider what this would do to Morton in his condition?" May asked to his back.

Tate stopped at the door and considered walking away without answering. The question felt rhetorical. But he turned, looked at his feet to think the thought through carefully and to get his words right.

Then he looked at her and held her gaze. "I considered a lot of things, May. And I decided to give a man and his son the opportunity to say goodbye."

Willow jumped from her chair, gave May a quick hug, and strode to Tate's side, taking his arm. "You going to his room?"

Tate nodded, feeling like a fist was stuck in his throat.

"I'll go with you," she said. "You want to come, Aunt May?"

May rose on a sigh. "I'm not sitting here alone waiting for that rat bastard to show up."

CHAPTER TWENTY-ONE

BUNNY FOUND THE COLORFULLY PAINTED rock easily enough, but laughed to herself when she noticed that the design was made up of neither flowers nor butterflies, but of ladybugs and toadstools.

Once she let herself in she perused the kitchen counter and other surfaces for something that looked like the list of names she needed to find. She hoped to save Tate the trouble of walking her through the search himself.

In the living room, she found a piano and antique desk with a roll top that was open. Her eye was drawn to the framed photos standing on the piano top, and despite a part of her that told her not to snoop, she moved close enough to inspect them anyway.

A black and white photo in a black wooden eight by ten frame stood taller than the rest amidst an array of color photographs. It was a shot of Tate and Jill.

They were very young, and she guessed it could have been their engagement portrait—it definitely had a professional touch. Jill, with her straight hair that lifted lightly on a breeze. Her smile was natural, honest, and content.

A clean shaven Tate, arms wrapped around her from the side, appeared captivated by her. Adoring her. His absorption was so deep that Bunny imagined a hundred bombs could have detonated around them, and he wouldn't have even flinched from his reverence.

The truth of it felt like a punch to Bunny's gut. The portrait spoke volumes and told Bunny all she needed to know. Jill had owned all of his heart. She wondered if there was any left for someone else.

She allowed her gaze to travel quickly over the other pictures—Tate and Jill, Tate and Willow, Tate and Jill and Willow—before tearing herself away. She shouldn't have snooped. Bad idea. Or, maybe it was good that she had. Better to understand now before she allowed herself to be hurt again.

She walked back into the kitchen, pulled her cell phone from her purse and dialed.

"Hi. It's Bunny. I'm at your place in the kitchen. Where should I look?"

"Um, let me think..." Tate's voice was deeper than usual. He sounded tired. "If you go into the living room, you'll see a desk."

She pretended like she hadn't already seen it. "Okay. Right. I see it. The top is rolled back."

"Great. Look for a steno pad with yellow paper. You know—like a secretary would use."

Bunny held the phone with one hand and moved papers around with the other. She recognized some of the papers as the same fliers she had at home for high school events and announcements. "There's a blue spiral notebook here. Is that it?"

"No. This would be smaller than that. It should have rings at the top. Brown cover maybe. You can open the drawers. I might have stuffed it in one of those."

She pulled open one drawer and then the other without any luck. "I'm sorry. It's not here."

"Okay, scratch the desk. Could you try the bookshelf in my bedroom then? I tend to stash things there."

"Sure." Under different circumstances, she would have considered making some little joke about his bedroom and the fun they'd had there the night before. But his father was dying, and she'd just figured out that a ghost had probably been with them in the room last night. A ghost she'd never be able to compete with. No, she wouldn't be making any jokes.

She did, though, enjoy the smell of him as she entered his room. The two bookshelves were side-by-side on the wall just to the left of the door. She scanned the shelves.

"How are you, by the way?" he asked her.

"Me? I should be asking you that question."

"You said you were having father issues."

"Oh, that." She laughed a little while lifting some more papers on a shelf right in front of her eyes. "You have your long stories, and I have mine."

She fingered the spines of his books. *Walden* by Henry David Thoreau, *Nature* by Ralph Waldo Emerson, *My First Summer in the Sierra*, *The Yosemite*, and *Travels in Alaska* by John Muir.

The titles were no surprise. They were perched next to rows and rows of novels by names she knew very well—Robert Heinlein, Isaac Asimov, Philip K. Dick, and more. Daddy loved science fiction too, not surprising, given his new passion for killing imaginary aliens.

"You're a science fiction fan," she said.

"What?"

"Your books. Sorry, I was looking at a few of them when I should be looking for that steno pad. Which I'm not finding by the way. Anywhere else?"

"Go around the corner on the other side of the bookshelves. There's a small sitting room with a TV. Is it on the chair or maybe on the table next to it?"

She looked. "Nope."

"Man. Really?" Tate said. Bunny imagined him running his hands through his hair in frustration. "I was sure I'd put it on the desk or on the bookshelf." He went quiet again, and Bunny tried to think of ways she could help better. "I guess I'll just have to call Hildie," he said.

Forget Hildie Page. Bunny could handle this. She wanted to handle this. "Don't bother Hildie. I can be here tomorrow if the kids know what to do. Is that all you need, or do they require instructions?"

"No instruction needed. It will be three hours or so. Are you sure?"

"I'll bring a book. Or maybe borrow your *Ender's Game*—if that would be okay. I've always wanted to read it. No reason for everything to get behind schedule, right?"

"Yeah. That's great. And definitely—borrow the book. Keep it as long as you like. I told the kids to be there at one. You're sure about this?"

"Positive. Go now, and don't worry about anything here."

"I'll, uh, call tomorrow. You know—when I have a better idea about how things are going here. Not sure if I'll be back for work on Monday or not."

Bunny worried about how to end the conversation. They'd shared a deeply intimate experience last night, and now just a few hours later, were discussing business as if they were merely acquaintances.

He was probably on the other end of the line kicking himself, wishing they hadn't slept together. "Okay. Bye," she said. There, that was the easy way out.

He didn't respond immediately.

She closed her eyes, breathed in the masculine scent around her, and prayed he'd say something that told her he wasn't regretting their night together.

"Yeah," he said finally. "Bye."

CHAPTER TWENTY-TWO

SAMUEL'S TEXT CAME IN WHILE a doctor discussed Morton's current condition with Tate and May. Their brother was waiting in the first floor lounge.

Tate tried to stay focused on the doctor's recommendations. Morton had likely come into contact with a flu bug, hence the high fever. With a highly compromised immune system, his body didn't fight it well. They'd brought the fever down a good deal, but wanted to keep him at least another day to monitor him.

"His chart shows he hasn't received any chemotherapy treatments, is that correct?"

Tate nodded. "He rejected the treatment when the diagnosis was made. He's, uh, basically..."

"Waiting to die," May finished for him.

The doctor nodded. "I see."

Tate helped the doctor understand the big picture. "We have a nurse with him part-time for right now. He has his good days and his bad. We know that at some point we will have to bring hospice in." He hesitated for a minute. "Do you think we're at that point now?"

"It could be."

"Will you be able to release him so we can take him home? We live in Virginia, you know."

"If we get to that point, I, or one of my associates will likely recommend medical transport. Highly recommend."

"Meaning, you don't release him if he doesn't have it?"

"Let's see what tomorrow brings."

Tate nodded, while May tapped her hand nervously against her leg. "Fair enough," Tate said.

Tate and May exchanged looks, and then Tate popped his head into Morton's room where Willow sat in a chair next to his bed.

The old man stared at a television.

Tate motioned to Willow that she should leave the room. "Hey, Mort," he said, "the doctor filled you in, right? Your fever is coming down."

"I don't wanna die in this hospital." The mere sliver of the man he knew as his father never took his eyes from the television as he rasped his words. "Take me home."

"We're working on that."

"Work harder." Morton coughed a dry, harsh cough.

"Can I get you something before we go down to the cafeteria?"

"A ticket home—you able to get me that?"

Tate bit his lip. If the man hadn't been so adamant about going to North Carolina in the first place, they wouldn't all be in this pickle now. He'd love to scream at Morton and tell him he wanted to be home just as badly. It served him right if he died in the hospital. He shook off the urge and concentrated, instead, on the more uncomfortable thought of seeing Samuel.

"We'll see you later, Mort."

Not surprisingly, Mort didn't look at him or answer.

May refused to see Samuel. She huffed off to the cafeteria while Tate and Willow took the elevator to the first floor.

When the doors opened, Tate felt the urge to punch the *Close Doors* button. Probably sensing his reluctance, Willow put her hand gently around his arm and pulled.

How do you greet someone you haven't seen in over thirty years? Someone you barely remember, but who shares your blood, your DNA? Someone who left you and never cared to come back.

From the doorway leading into the first floor lounge, it wasn't hard to spot Samuel—he was the only one sitting there. His hair was thin, more gray than dusty brown. It was cut short and business conservative. He had the Kilbourn brown eyes. Despite their casual flair, his pants and shirt were obviously designer and probably cost more than most of Tate's wardrobe put together.

He was focused on a computer tablet in his hand, but raised his head as soon as Tate and Willow appeared in the doorway. Samuel's motions were slow and deliberate. He set the tablet on the chair next to him, rose, and then took tentative steps in Tate's direction.

Tate managed one step into the lounge and, as unsmiling as Samuel, took his brother's offered hand.

"Tate," his brother said. A statement, not a question.

Tate shook his hand, but said nothing.

"Thank you for calling me. And for inviting me to come down."

"You didn't need an invitation."

Samuel tipped his head, and Tate could hear the silent *touché*. He put his arm around Willow's shoulder. "This is my daughter, Willow."

Tate saw Willow smile and offer her hand willingly. "Hi," she said.

"Nice to meet you, Willow." Samuel cleared his throat after the handshake and thrust his hand into his pants pocket. "May isn't here?"

"She wasn't up for it—the reunion, if you will."

"Got it. Understand." Samuel's gaze fell to his feet. "How about...Dad?"

Willow muffled a laugh with her hand, and Tate couldn't help but crack a small smile.

"Uh, Morton doesn't know that you're here." Then it occurred to him that he may have misunderstood. "Or were you asking about how he's doing?"

"Both, I suppose."

"His fever is coming down, but they want to keep him here at least overnight. Morton wants to go home and is..." Tate's voice trailed off. How could he put it nicely?

"Grumpier than usual," Willow offered.

Tate nodded. "Grumpier than usual."

"So." Samuel bobbed his head. "Not up for a visit from the son he hasn't seen in thirty-four years?"

"Probably not."

Samuel nodded and when he did, Tate noticed some of Morton in the action. Odd, he thought, that mannerisms would hold strong after so long. He wondered if they were alike in other ways.

"So," Samuel started again, "Morton, huh? His idea or yours?"

"The name?" Tate asked rhetorically. He shrugged. "Happened over time, I guess." He tried to remember who started the habit of referring to their father by his given name. Was it him or May? Probably May.

It must have happened shortly after Samuel left though, because Tate had a very vivid memory of apologizing to his third grade teacher when his father didn't show up for a scheduled teacher/parent conference. "Morton was probably busy with work and couldn't get away," Tate had said.

"You call your father Morton?" she'd asked. When Tate said yes, the teacher shook her head and told Tate that he should never apologize to her for his father's neglect.

He didn't know what neglect meant for certain, so he looked it up in the dictionary during library time the next day. He was surprised at the word's meaning. Certainly he envied the kids with two parents who showed up to school events and actually seemed interested, but he had never considered himself neglected.

His father worked and paid the bills and "put food on the table" and "clothes on their backs" as the man reminded he and May quite regularly.

It wasn't until middle school that he began to realize that good parenting meant more than providing food and shelter. He finally realized that Morton had given up. He'd given up on all of them, himself included, and even then, he was just waiting to die.

It was during those same years—middle school and high school—that Tate made the conscious decision to be a different man. He wouldn't let his father's misery define him. He'd be better that. He would find the fun and joy in life. And when he had kids, he'd be a damn good father.

May's voice behind him startled Tate from his jog down memory lane.

"You know I hate you, you bloody rat bastard," she said, her voice quavering.

Tate turned to see May, hands at her sides, face red, eyes wet.

Willow took a step backward, and Tate could tell she was concerned for her aunt. Samuel and May stood motionless, locked in a visual stand-off. Neither spoke. Their eyes did all of the talking.

"Say it," May whispered finally.

Samuel watched her intently and finally responded. "They're only words, May, but if it helps...I'm sorry?"

"Are you bloody asking me or telling me?"

"I'm sorry."

Because his sister's emotions rollercoasted like Space Mountain, Tate wasn't surprised when May wrapped herself tightly around Samuel and began bawling like a baby.

"I hate you." Her words were barely audible.

Samuel hugged his sister back, stroking her hair. "Not more than I hate myself."

All this time, Tate had worried that his motives for contacting Samuel were selfish. And maybe they were. But here, in this cold hospital lounge, he felt relieved to see that he'd done the right thing. Selfish or not, he'd done the right thing.

CHAPTER TWENTY-THREE

BUNNY UNLOCKED THE FRONT DOOR of the Nature Center at eight forty-five and told her father to take a seat in the learning cove where the naturalists gave their presentations. Luckily, Demon had been unable to shut down his access to the bank account even though she was a joint owner.

Bunny and her dad had been able to purchase an iPad to keep him occupied while they put their plan in order to get him safely and happily back into his apartment at Whispering Pines.

"Daddy, just sit there quietly. When my boss comes in, I'll ask her for a long lunch break." Bunny's nerves were in a knot. She'd only been working at the Nature Center for a couple of weeks. She didn't want to jeopardize the new job that she loved, but she also needed to help Daddy extricate himself from the clutches of a daughter who'd taken his trust too far.

Over the weekend, the only time she didn't have Daddy with her was when she'd gone to Tate's looking for the steno pad. Even then, she had left him with Charlie at the electronics superstore where they sampled video gaming units and games for more than two hours.

While she waited for Abigail to arrive, she listened to messages and then went to the kitchen to make a pot of coffee. She was still wound pretty tight, so the coffee would be for her co-workers. She poured herself a mug of cold water from the cooler, instead.

She walked around the Center turning on lights, then returned to her desk just as Lydia entered, followed by Ross—the two naturalists under Tate's supervision.

They smiled and waved at Bunny.

"Hi guys," she said. "Tate asked me to let you know he won't be in today. He's had a family emergency."

Concern crossed both of their faces. "Is everything okay?" Lydia asked.

"It's his father," Bunny explained. "He got sick during a trip to North Carolina and had to be hospitalized." Tate had warned Bunny that no one at the Center knew of his father's cancer, and he wanted to keep it that way for the time being, anyway.

She kept talking, offering as much as she could in the way of information, hoping they wouldn't ask questions she couldn't answer. "He's expecting the hospital to release him soon, and he'll call as soon as he knows when he'll be back."

Luckily, the phone rang, rescuing her. "Oh, he said to call him on his cell phone if you need him for anything urgent." She picked up the ringing phone, leaving Lydia and Ross to wander back to their offices, discussing the news.

She handled the phone call and was just hanging up when Abigail arrived, Olga on her heels. "Abigail," Bunny said, trying not to sound as worried as she felt, "can I talk to you for a few minutes?"

A floral tote dangled from Abigail's left hand, and her right thumb was tucked into the straps of a very large brown purse flung over her other shoulder. She seemed a bit burdened by the tote. "Is this urgent, Bunny?" she asked, a hint of irritation in her voice.

Bunny felt that Abigail had really warmed up to her over the last couple of weeks, and she hoped that the irritation was just a by-product of morning grumpies and a heavy book bag pulling on her arm.

"It's pretty urgent, yes," answered Bunny.

Olga sidled up to Abigail.

Bunny didn't mind if Olga heard about her problem. She considered Olga a friend of sorts by now.

Abigail dropped the floral bag to the floor and leaned on the tall counter of the reception desk. "What is it?" She looked serious for a minute, then actually cracked a smile. "You don't want a raise already, do you?"

Bunny returned the smile. "No, but I do have a pretty big favor to ask."

"Aha! Gotcha!" her father's voice boomed loudly from the Learning Cove, causing Bunny to wince. She was glad he had games to play on his iPad, but did he have to be so loud?

"That's the favor," she said. "Rather, that's my dad. He needs me to take him to the courthouse today to apply for an emergency restraining order. I thought if I took a long lunch..."

"Restraining order for what?" Abigail seemed genuinely concerned.

Good, Bunny thought, maybe she'd be fine with it.

"Who cares for what? None of our business!" blurted Olga. "Abigail, I answer phones. You let Bunny do thees for her papa. It sounds serious."

Abigail gave Olga a sideways glance. "Do you promise not to yell at people?"

"Who yell? I don't yell?" Olga yelled. It was true, Olga talked quite loudly and some took her enthusiasm for shouting.

Abigail rolled her eyes. "How long will you be gone?" she asked Bunny.

"It should only take a few minutes to file the paperwork, so I'm thinking with waiting for the approval and travel time, two hours at the most. But," she winced again, deciding to go ahead and approach the full scope of the problem head-on, "this is only a temporary order so I'll have to take him back for a court date later this week or early next, and that could take a big chunk of the day. My sister will probably have some big hired guns in there fighting him hard. She's married to the big developer, Randall Strickland."

Olga let out a belly laugh, and Abigail's mouth tightened into a thinner-than-usual line. "Wait. You mean Deena Hobbs-Strickland is your sister?"

Bunny worried that she'd just ruined it for herself and Daddy. Why did Deena have to have everyone in her back pocket? She nodded, her face tight.

"You take as much time as you need, Bunny." Abigail slammed a fist on the counter. "If I had a lawyer to send with you, I would. Deena Hobbs-Strickland is no friend to the Nature Center.

"Olga, you watch the phones for Bunny so she can go now and get this taken care of. No reason to wait for lunch."

Abigail picked up her floral tote, muttering to herself all the way to her office.

Olga scooted around to Bunny's side of the desk. "In Abigail's book, the Devil hisself has more goodness in his heart than Deena-Hobbs Strickland. You have heard about the big petition?"

Bunny picked up her purse, thankful that she could get this business done now. "What petition?"

"To cut funding to Nature Center. She has proposal to build new shopping center on Lake Emerson. Many people make the jokes, but lots of truth in joking, that she has plans for statue to be erected in this shopping center if gets built."

"Statue of what?"

"Herself, of course. Like I say, it's the joking, but who knows, eh?" Olga hopped up into Bunny's rolling chair. Her legs dangled, not touching the floor. She made a shooing gesture at Bunny. "Make the skedaddling."

The restraining order—or protection order as the form called it—was simple to get. Nothing more was required than an application and approval.

Once they were done, Daddy had a piece of paper to protect him from Deena's attempt to remove him from his apartment. The nice courthouse clerk said the order would protect him from any of Deena's tricks in the short term.

With the protection order in his hand and a new pay-as-you-go cell phone from the electronics store, Daddy felt in control. "I want to go back to my apartment now," he said.

"Are you sure, Daddy?"

"I'm very sure. Not gonna let her keep me scared. Learned my lesson. Gotta talk to my buddy Walter, anyway. See if his son can represent me in this whole mess."

"I'm worried about you."

"Nah." He patted her hand. "I'm a grown man. I can take care of myself."

"A grown man that somehow let his daughter hold him hostage against his will?"

"I said I learned my lesson."

Bunny tried not to pout. "I like having you around."

"Jeezy Lou, Bunny Cakes," he said, "You'd get tired of me just as fast as I'd get tired of you."

He was probably right, Bunny thought. With his new obsession for video games, it would be like having another teenage boy in the house.

Yet, he had been a savior the day before, helping the boys and girls paint sets in Tate's garage. He'd seemed to enjoy himself.

She got out of the car and walked with Daddy to the lobby of Whispering Pines. "Daddy," she said, "I could use more help with the sets for the play. My friend might be gone for a few more days, and even when he gets back I think he's going to be occupied with other things. Would it be okay if I told him you and I could help out—take over if necessary?"

Daddy nodded. "That's a great idea. And maybe some of my buddies could chip in. Harry was a contractor. Should I talk to him?"

"That would be great." She hugged him tight.

Nice Nancy's eyes nearly bulged out of her sockets when she saw them approach the desk.

Bunny's father slapped the official document onto the shiny granite counter top. "Get Dan Baker here. I want him to see this right now."

Nancy shifted her eyes back and forth between Bunny and her father. She leaned over the desk and whispered, "She's here with the police."

As if on cue, Demon's voice echoed loudly from around the corner at the end of the large foyer of Whispering Pines. "My husband, Randall Strickland, and I are very concerned and expect the Rustic Woods Police to make sure my father is returned safely, Officer White. You understand that my father, Douglas Hobbs, is highly respected in this community. He once owned all eight Peppy's Pizza restaurants in Fairfax county and sat on the Rustic Woods Homeowners Association board for three years."

Bunny watched Demon, the police officer, and Dan Baker all round the corner. "Yes, you've mentioned that fact several times now," the officer said to Demon.

Demon shouted and pointed when she spotted Bunny and her father standing in the lobby. "That's them! Arrest her officer! She put my poor sweet father in danger!"

Daddy snatched the paper from the desk and held it in the air with both hands as if he were holding up a poster at a protest rally. "I got a protection order. You're not arresting anyone today, sir!"

"That's correct," the police officer said, strolling their way, a hand resting relaxed on his holstered gun. "We aren't arresting anyone today...Mr. Hobbs, is it?"

"That's right. And this is my other daughter Bunny who rescued me from confinement on Saturday. I'm not the one with mental problems here."

"No one is accusing you of having mental problems, Mr. Hobbs."

The officer gave Bunny a tip of the head and small smile that made her relax the tiniest bit. "You are Ms…" he looked at his note pad. "Ms. Bergen?"

She nodded. She felt the lump in her throat that often made her voice quaver when she got nervous, but she made a conscious effort to think that lump away. "Yes," she said, pleased when her vocal chords obeyed. "I am Ms. Bergen, Douglas Hobbs' younger daughter."

"Can I see that paper in your hands, Mr. Hobbs?"

Daddy handed it over reluctantly. "Make sure I get it back."

Demon made an attempt at running toward them, but her large bulk didn't move too quickly.

Officer White gestured her back. "Don't come any closer, Mrs. Strickland." He continued to inspect the document.

Demon didn't seem to care about being ordered to stay back. "It's Hobbs-Strickland, and—"

Officer White turned back to her. "Halt now, or I'll be forced to place you under arrest."

That stopped Demon. She was rarely confused or off-balance, but that's exactly how she looked now. "I don't understand. What's happening here?"

Officer White handed the paper back to Daddy and stepped back toward Demon. "Your father has obtained an emergency protection order against you, Mrs. Hobbs-Strickland."

"Against me?" she shouted. She pointed to Bunny. "She's the one—"

"I will walk you outside of the premises, Mrs. Strickland."

"Hobbs-Strickland," she protested.

"I will walk you outside of the premises and explain the law, as it applies to you currently." He put a hand near, but not on Demon's back, guiding her toward the automatic doors.

He glanced over his shoulder toward Dan Baker, who had been observing the hubbub with nearly the same amount of confusion as Demon. "Mr. Baker, please see that Mr. Hobbs returns safely to his unit and that you do due diligence in seeing that order is enforced."

Dan Baker nodded.

Demon could be heard shouting threats to Officer White all the way out those sliding glass doors, and Bunny wondered if her sister wouldn't manage to get herself arrested anyway.

Bunny smiled. Not because she was happy to see her sister brought to heel (although that did give her momentary pleasure), but because she had stood strong. Things, she thought, were beginning to turn around for her.

At least, she hoped this was just the beginning of good things to come.

CHAPTER TWENTY-FOUR

Monday afternoon, Tate decided that Willow shouldn't miss any more school, so May agreed to drive her back to Rustic Woods. May would go back to her job in Washington, D.C. and then drive back to Virginia each night to stay with Willow until Tate and Samuel were able to bring Morton home.

By Wednesday morning, Tate was tired of the small hotel room, the bad food, and the restless nights. The static air that still hung between he and Samuel wasn't pleasant either.

Neither of them seemed very good at starting conversations, or once some words were exchanged, they couldn't seem to keep the momentum going.

Tate did learn that Samuel, like May, had never married or had kids. Samuel blamed the overwhelming nature of his business life, but Tate posited that their own circumstances growing up certainly hadn't been a valuable lesson in how to get married, have kids, and live happily ever after.

Samuel also admitted that he knew Tate had married. He said he had even talked once with Jill on the phone when they lived in California, but had chickened out at the last minute and pretended to be a telemarketer. That, he said, was the one and only time he had tried to contact Tate.

Samuel was waiting for Tate in the hospital lounge when he walked in.

"Have you seen a doctor yet?" Tate asked him.

Samuel shook his head. "No. I just got here. You should be the one to talk to them."

Tate nodded, tucking the leather portfolio filled with his father's medical documentation and insurance notes under one arm. He was hoping that the doctors would finally agree to let Morton go home. His fever had come down the previous day, and his pain was being managed with drugs.

Upstairs, far enough from the room so Morton couldn't see or hear, the doctor reviewed Morton's case with Tate and Samuel. "We have been talking with both the oncologist on site as well as your father's doctor and oncologist back home. Your father continues to reject a chemotherapy option that could possibly extend his life another three, possibly four months."

Tate nodded.

"At this point," the doctor continued, "your father has seen some improvement, but the pain needs management, and he should be on oxygen. There's some incontinence as well. We will recommend release to hospice care in his home, but suggest that he be transported by ambulance with a team on board to maintain his comfort for the long distance."

"What will that cost?" Tate asked.

"I'm going to have you work with a woman in our administrative office. She'll put you in contact with the company and they will discuss cost, insurance, billing—all of the particulars."

Tate dropped his head in frustration. That meant another day of paperwork, waiting on hold for a "health care advocate" who was never an advocate of anything but insurance company policy. The advocate would probably get on the phone, and then transfer him to five more "advocates."

Samuel rested a hand on Tate's shoulder. "You're tired. Let me handle this."

That would be nice, Tate thought. Nice for someone else to manage this bloody crap for a while. He smiled at his own inner sister. "I don't know..."

"Is everything I need in there?" Samuel pointed to the portfolio in Tate's hand.

"Yeah." Tate considered the offer. He did need to call into work, check on things, and let Bunny know what to tell everyone. He handed the portfolio over, thankful for the reprieve. "I'll be outside. I need to call work and check in. Text me if you need anything."

It was a cold March morning, and a misty rain made the air feel even colder. Tate had come outside to give a grieving family some privacy.

He dialed Bunny's cell phone. He didn't want to deal with someone else who might pick up the Nature Center phone if she happened to be away from the desk when he called.

"Hello?" she answered.

"Hey. It's me."

"I know." He could hear the smile in her voice, and that made the rain feel less depressing. "I'm at the front desk," she whispered, "so I'm trying to sound very business-like."

"You're doing a good job of it."

"How is your dad?"

"Better. We're working out a way to get him home right now. I don't know what that entails. I might be back today or tomorrow...or who knows."

"That sounds promising."

Tate couldn't help but smile just hearing her voice, but also her tone. She always seemed to be looking for the positive. "I think so. I'll call when I know more, but for right now, obviously I'm not coming in today."

"I'll tell everyone. They're worried about you, and Lydia and Ross wanted to send flowers to the hospital. Can I give them that information at least?"

"No. Morton could care less. It's a nice idea, and tell them I said thank you for the thought."

"I think they just want to show support for you."

"I know." He closed his eyes and imagined Bunny in her chair talking into the phone. Maybe she was twisting a pen between two fingers like she did when she was on the phone handling business. Or tucking her hair behind her ears and leaning her chin in her hand the way he had seen her do over the last couple of weeks.

Then he pictured her lying in his bed next to him and could almost feel the touch of her soft skin against his.

He opened his eyes at the sound of the hospital doors opening. A couple walked past him, opening their umbrellas to the rain. "How are you?" he asked Bunny.

"Good. I was able to reach everyone on the set crew like you asked. They'll be moving everything from your garage to my garage on Saturday. I have everyone's email addresses now, too."

"That's great. And you're sure about this?"

"Are you kidding me? Daddy is very excited. He's been recruiting some guys from the Pines. I'll have food there, and they'll just take over where you started. One less worry on your plate. Charlie said he'll tell Ms. Steffler that everything is being taken care of."

"I think I'll owe you at least a dinner out when this is all over." The words were out of his mouth before he could stop them.

"Oh, you don't owe me anything..." She seemed to be hesitating. "But that would be nice anyway. Should I check in on Willow for you?"

"May texted me last night. They changed her work schedule so she's home today."

He didn't want to get off the phone, and yet he did. He didn't like talking, and yet he could talk to her all day long. He heard the Nature Center phone ring in the background, and he knew he didn't have a choice. "I hear your phone—go ahead and take that. I'll call when I know more."

"Okay. Have a good..." she stopped herself midway through her usual sign-off. "I mean, take care."

By late afternoon, all plans had been made for Morton's transport home. A hospital bed had been rented and would be delivered Thursday morning, about the same time that Morton would begin his ambulance ride back to Virginia. A nurse would arrive Thursday afternoon to meet Morton and the family.

Samuel went back to the hotel to get some work done while Tate sat down with Mort to explain.

The old man reached for his cup of water.

Tate helped him, taking the cup and holding it so his father could drink from the straw. He was weak, and Tate could see that even sucking on the straw was taxing his energy.

When he'd had enough, he pushed Tate's hand away, not bothering to say thank you.

Tate would have been shocked if Morton had uttered any appreciation. It would have been a sure sign that Tate was in the wrong room or that a pod-Morton had been put in his place. "Good news," Tate said. "You're going home tomorrow."

"Why not now?"

"You'll be going by ambulance, and you'll have a comfortable hospital bed there waiting for you."

"How's that gonna happen?"

"May is letting them in." That, in fact, was a lie. He and Samuel had already decided that since May had to work, Samuel would fly up early in the morning and get the house ready.

Morton winced, squeezing his eyes shut. He was pale, and his eyelids looked as thin as rice paper.

"You okay?" Tate asked him.

"Feel like shit."

"Can I do anything for you?"

"I suppose you're doing everything you can."

Tate shrugged. "Do you want me to stay with you for a while?"

"Nah. I feel a sleep coming on. No need."

Tate gave a light pat to the side of Morton's bed. Morton had never been much for physical shows of affection, so Tate was pretty sure he wouldn't be up for a supportive pat or squeeze now. "I'll head out then. See you tomorrow morning."

Morton didn't open his eyes or otherwise acknowledge the goodbye.

Tate was walking through the door to leave when he heard his father's weak voice. "Where's the girl?"

He stopped and turned. "You mean Willow?"

Morton's nod was faint, but observable.

"She's with May back home. I thought I told you."

"She's going to be in that play, right?"

Chalk one up to Morton for throwing Tate a curve ball. He wasn't sure he'd even said anything to Mort about it. Maybe Willow had told him. "Yeah."

His father swallowed. "Good."

When Tate was pretty sure the conversation had ended, he left the hospital for the night.

Tate was resting on his hotel bed, propped against the headboard with pillows, and clicking the television remote when he heard a knock on the door. Reluctantly, he rose and padded to the door in his stocking feet.

The hotel near the hospital was a far cry from five-star quality, and the door handle required some jiggling to get it work. Such a door was not the safest in the event of fire, he thought.

When he finally managed to get the door open, Samuel stood with a large pizza box in one hand and a six-pack of bottled beer in the other.

A smile tugged at the corner of Tate's mouth. "Dos Equiis?"

Samuel shook his head. "Asahi."

"Asa-what?"

"Asahi. It's Japanese. You have a problem with that?"

Tate stepped back, making way for his brother to enter the small room. "I'm many things, but not a beer snob. I am a pizza snob though. What kind of toppings did you put on that thing?" He grabbed the remote and clicked the television off.

"Grease. They appear to have put a lot of grease on it. That, and sausage, mushrooms, and hot peppers."

Tate let a furrow crease his brow. "How did you know?"

"I called Willow. She claims you won't touch a pizza with any other toppings."

"I don't."

"Good thing I called her then, huh?"

"Or you could have just called me." To his own ears, Tate's response sounded harsh, and he regretted it immediately.

But Samuel didn't flinch. "It wouldn't have been a surprise then, would it? Where should I put it? This thing is still hot."

Tate pointed to the double bed that had been Willow's, then relieved Samuel of the six-pack. He set it on the dresser, removed two of the bottles, and unscrewed the tops.

He took a swig from one. Nice choice. Good, sharp flavor. His brother had good taste in beer.

He handed Samuel the other bottle. "Have a seat. And thanks. I wasn't really up for going out."

Samuel repositioned the desk chair and sat. "Me either." He pulled a long and hard swig on his beer before setting it down on the desk and reaching for a slice of pizza. "So, what was his story about why I left?"

Just ready to shove the corner of his pizza slice into his mouth, Tate stopped. The pizza, the beer. He got it now. They were the ice breaker for *the talk*.

Tate proceeded to bite and chew, giving himself time to answer. He was hungry, and the pizza, despite the grease, looked and smelled delicious. He chased the spicy bite with a sip of beer. "He said you fought over money."

"I figured as much," Samuel said around his own mouthful. "Nothing else?"

"Just that you asked for a loan to pay for your last semester." The story had seemed plausible. Even as a young child, Tate was aware that money was a sore spot between both May and Samuel and their dad. Mort had told them that his own parents hadn't paid for his college education, and he wouldn't pay for theirs. Never mind that he could well-afford to send six or seven kids to college.

Working to pay your way through college builds character, he had said. Then, of course, when Tate was entering his college application phase of life, he lived through the same lectures himself. He already knew, seeing Samuel and May struggle, that Morton wasn't going to fork over the bucks or the encouragement, but that didn't stop Morton from diving into a twenty minute dissertation on how "kids today" have everything handed to them on a silver platter and nothing comes free—everything needs to be earned with blood, sweat, and tears. About the twentieth time he'd heard the speech, Tate wanted to draw some blood alright, but not his own.

Because his father had more than sufficient income, Tate was forced to seek merit scholarships, which were hard to come by, and to take out high interest loans. On-campus jobs went to work-study students first, so he often had to find menial jobs off-campus.

Did he learn to work hard? Absolutely. But he also learned indifference toward a man who, in his mind, was only a father by decree of a birth certificate.

And that was why Tate never returned home after leaving for college. He had left Rustic Woods in body and spirit. Only he hadn't left a six year-old brother behind the way Samuel had done. A brother who worshiped him.

"I did ask for a loan," Samuel nodded, "and we argued about it. But that's not why I left."

Tate swallowed. "So, I suppose you left because you hated him. He has a way of putting people off, especially his kids."

"I found her journal."

The word "her" hit Tate like a one-two punch to the stomach, leaving him momentarily short of breath. He knew Samuel wasn't talking about May.

"Mom's journal?"

Samuel's head dropped, his eyes staring at the floor. "She was always more important to him than we were, you know."

No, he didn't know. How could he? He waited, knowing Samuel had far more to say.

"At the dinner table, he'd say to her, 'When we get these two money-suckers raised and out of the house, you and I can start living our life. I want to take you to Scotland.'" Samuel shook his head. "I don't remember if he said Scotland exactly, but there was always a place he was going to take her when May and I were out of his way and not sucking up his money anymore.

"She'd always yell at him, not angrily, but enough to let him know she didn't like it when he said things like that in front of us. I went to boy scout camp one summer. May said he didn't notice that I was gone for three days."

"An obvious nominee for Father of the Year," Tate joked, trying to add some levity to the depressing conversation. Samuel's account enlightening, though. May had never talked about this side of Morton.

Samuel laughed and took another pull on his beer. "When she was sick, before we knew it was cancer, he'd yell at us and blame us for stressing her out. She didn't seem sick, just tired. All of the time. I can't remember which we learned first—that she was pregnant or that she had cancer. It was a bad time. They fought a lot, and we didn't really understand what was happening until Mom finally sat us down to talk. You probably know all of this from May."

"Bits and pieces only. She's a talker, but not about that." Tate still wanted to hear about the journal, but he tried to be patient and let Samuel tell his side of the story in his own way.

"Did she talk about Mom at all?"

"Sure. Lots of stories. Funny stories. May said she was a funny lady."

Samuel's smile was unrestrained. "She was."

"Morton—not so funny. I guess opposites really do attract." Tate decided to press Samuel a bit. "So why did you leave? I mean, if you want to get that off your chest."

He stared at the bottle in his hand. "I resented you for leaving, I'll admit. But then again I got out of there as soon as I could, too."

"The journal. I read it. Then I confronted him and told him he was a sick bastard. In return, he told me he never wanted to see my ugly face again as long as he lived."

"But you don't want to tell me what was in it."

Samuel examined his beer bottle. A corner of the label had started to come up, and he worked it with his thumbnail while he spoke. "He begged her to have an abortion so she could do chemo. She wouldn't do it. She wanted you."

Tate didn't blink. His father had never wanted him. That wasn't a surprise. He didn't need a journal entry to tell him that. He leaned forward. "I'll be honest, I'm not sure how that was bad for you. Don't get me wrong, I...am glad I'm alive. But if she'd had an abortion, she might have survived, and you'd still have a mother. Didn't some part of you wish she had?" He marveled at his own ability to say those words so calmly.

Samuel finally took his eyes off the bottle and looked at Tate. "The old man told her if she didn't do it, then she obviously didn't love him at all, and that he'd hate her for the 'rest of her miserable life on earth.'" Samuel visibly choked back emotion. "Those were the words she wrote. And it all made sense looking back. I never saw him show her a single bit of affection toward the end of the pregnancy.

"He wasn't around when you were born. He wouldn't go near her when she died five months later. At the time, I thought it was just how he coped. Coping badly, but it wasn't out of character. But he wasn't coping. He was punishing. Punishing her. To the very bitter end, that asshole punished her for loving her kids."

"Then you're wrong on one point," Tate said.

Samuel shook his head, not understanding.

"You said he always cared more about her than his kids. If what you're saying is true, he didn't care about her at all. It was always about him."

They sat silently, but eventually, Tate had to speak up. "You didn't answer my question. Didn't you wish that she had ended the pregnancy and taken the chemotherapy?"

Samuel's gaze swiveled to the ceiling. His thumb tapped the beer bottle. He seemed to take forever in answering. "Yes, brother," he said finally. "I'm sorry to say that I wished it more than anything."

CHAPTER TWENTY-FIVE

$\mathcal{B}$UNNY'S EVENING WAS INTERESTING, TO say the least. It had started out wonderfully. She brought Daddy and his two friends, Harry and Jim, back to the house where they met a group of kids and volunteer parents.

The plan was to work on the set building in her garage. Daddy had paid for the sandwiches that she had ordered from the deli.

Everyone dug into the work, laughing and building. She put the radio on her favorite oldies station, and the kids danced while they painted. It looked like a scene from *The Big Chill*. Well, sort of. Oldies now included many of her favorite songs from the eighties. Talk about feeling old.

The phone rang somewhere between "Sweet Home Alabama" and "Love Shack." Bunny had to swallow a bite of tuna sandwich before answering. "Hello."

"Am I speaking with Mrs. Bergen?" a woman asked. The icy voice was familiar.

"This is Bunny."

"Regina Steffler."

"Oh," Bunny swallowed again. "Hi. How are you Ms. Steffler?" She cringed at the sound of her own quavering voice.

"I am concerned about Mr. Kilbourn's father and about our sets. I will be by shortly to see what sort of progress, if any, is being made. I do wish Mr. Kilbourn had taken a few moments to contact Mrs. Page rather than turning things over willy-nilly."

It sounded to Bunny like she was concerned about the sets and not so much about Tate's father. "That would be fine, Ms. Steffler." She motioned to her father to turn the music down. "I think you'll be pleased. Do you have the address?"

"I will see you soon, Mrs. Bergen."

Bunny heard the dial tone in her ear. "*Ms.* Bergen," she grumbled under her breath. "*Ms.*"

She set the walkabout handset down and clapped her hands to get everyone's attention. "Okay people, we have an inspection! Ms. Steffler is stopping by to see how things are coming along."

The workers barely paused long enough to listen to what Bunny had to say. As soon as she finished her announcement, they delved right back into sawing and hammering and painting.

Even with the cool air coming in from the open garage door, sweat dripped from her father's shiny head. He didn't seem worried. Bunny wished she could be as calm.

She thought about calling Tate for moral support, but reconsidered. He didn't need any more worries on his plate. She took a deep breath. It would all be fine. Daddy and the crew had done a beautiful job, and Steffler would be thrilled. Well, maybe not thrilled. The woman didn't look like she ever registered above *vaguely content* on any emotional scale.

If Bunny got a grunt of acceptance out of her, she'd consider it a victory.

Not ten minutes later, Bunny watched a black car pull into her driveway. It had to be Steffler. Given that the woman dressed entirely in black, of course her car would be black as well.

The arrival of a second car took her by surprise. From where she stood near the back of her garage, she couldn't see who was getting out.

Scooting around people and sawhorses, she made her way toward the visitors. She concentrated on her breathing and thinking happy thoughts, but when her gaze fell on Hildie Page, teetering on high heels next to a sullen Steffler, those happy thoughts flew out the window.

But Bunny refused to let her smile slip.

Outside on the driveway, Bunny shivered against the dark chilly night, and she could see her breath when she greeted the two women. "It's nice to see you again, Ms. Steffler. You too, Hild—" she stopped herself short, realizing she should be more formal. "Mrs. Page."

Right away, Hildie Page was all smiles and seemingly genuine pleasantness. "Nice to see you too, Bunny. And really, call me Hildie." She rested a thin, cold hand on Bunny's arm. "We're all friends here. I can't tell you how thankful we are that you were able to take over in this capacity, what with Mr. Kilbourn's family issues. You're a show saver, I must say."

"Where are the plans?" Steffler inquired. "I don't see the plans." Her squinty eyes darted all over the place.

"Oh, they're right here," Bunny said, guiding them to a part of the garage wall covered in the designs Tate had drawn up. "My daddy took over right where Tate...um, Mr. Kilbourn, left off." She waved a hand in the air to catch her father's attention. "Daddy. Harry. Could you come over here for a minute?"

"Daddy?" Steffler sniffed.

Bunny's first reaction was to apologize. Then she decided doing so was silly. Apologize for what? "I never stopped calling him Daddy. Term of endearment and all that."

Hildie smiled broadly, and Ms. Steffler remained thin-lipped. They both inspected the plans while the new team leaders made their way from one corner.

"Someone wants to inspect my work?" Daddy grumped, wiping sweat from his brow with an old handkerchief. "Who would that be?"

"Daddy," Bunny said, working hard to keep the conversation upbeat, "this is Ms. Steffler, the director of the play."

He didn't offer a hand, but he nodded. "Pleased to make your acquaintance. This is my friend Harry. He was a contractor before he retired. His son still owns the business. He knows his stuff."

"Is there something I can call you other than Daddy? A real name, perchance?"

"My wife used to call me, 'Hey You,' but you can call me Doug." Bunny had to fight against rolling her eyes when her father delivered his standard quip. The problem was, she knew he wasn't done.

"I'll answer to just about anything," he continued, "so long as it's nice."

Neither Hildie nor Ms. Steffler seemed to have a quick comeback so Daddy kept rolling. "We've done a good job here. We're on schedule, and we'll deliver a dandy set for you, and while I'm sure you're very thankful, I want to thank *you*."

Steffler blinked. "You want to thank me? For what?"

"Giving a few old men something to do. And these kids are great. I haven't had this much fun in a long time. How about you, Harry?"

Harry nodded his bald head in agreement. "Glad to be here helping out."

"More fun than we have killing aliens," Daddy added. "So you know it has to be good."

Bunny thought she saw the beginning of a smile on Steffler's stiff lip.

"Um," Bunny stepped in, "they play video games. They're, you know, not real aliens." That didn't sound as smart as it did in her head.

"So, Doug and Harry," Steffler said, pulling black leather gloves off her hands one finger at a time. "Show me what you've done, would you? I have high standards for my musicals." Her words were tough, but Bunny could see that Steffler was warming up to the men.

She followed the two, leaving Bunny and Hildie alone.

"Bunny," Hildie started in, "I want you to know that we are so grateful for you stepping up like this—"

"I know," Bunny interrupted her, "you already told me."

"But this really isn't your...you know...your thing. When I heard about Tate's problems, in my job as the volunteer coordinator, I quickly found someone else better suited to complete the job."

"What do you mean, this isn't my thing?"

"Your responsibility, I mean. It isn't your responsibility." Hildie did that thing again where she laid her hand on Bunny's arm, and Bunny knew she was being patronized. "But never fear, I have rescued you, and tomorrow this will no longer be your problem."

"It's not a problem, Hildie, and I'm managing fine. I like the responsibility. I don't see a reason to move the whole operation when it's working very well here."

"Well, is it? Really though?"

"Yes. Really." Bunny could feel her hands start to shake.

"You have enough problems, what with being out of work and everything."

"I'm not out of work."

"Oh." Hildie was obviously caught off-guard. "But my husband—I mean, he told me he had to let you go."

Bunny kept her voice low enough so that only Hildie could hear. "And you know what? Thank goodness for small miracles. If he hadn't had to...let me go..." She let the words sink in while Hildie's eyes batted a million times a minute. "If he hadn't had to let me go, I wouldn't have found my new job at the Nature Center. Better pay, better benefits. Really nice people. And I get to work with Tate Kilbourn."

Bunny thought Hildie might pop a few blood vessels, trying to keep her fake smile plastered on her face.

"Well..." Hildie didn't seem able to complete her thought.

So Bunny completed it for her. "You—I mean, your husband—actually did me a favor. Please thank him for me tonight, would you?" Then she leaned in more closely and whispered, "And by the way, my definition of a skank is a married woman who throws herself at single men."

Bunny had never, in her entire life, ever managed to deliver a deserving zinger at someone like Hildie Page. If she could have, she would have jumped for joy and shouted to the heavens, but the moment demanded decorum. And maybe a shot of whiskey afterwards to calm herself. Because, while she may have looked as placid as a calm summer lake on the outside, she was a bundle of jumpy nerves on the inside.

Daddy, Harry, and Regina Steffler returned, and all three of them were laughing. Bunny couldn't believe her eyes.

"You two are the best grandparent volunteers I've ever had," Ms. Steffler said to the two men. "Thank you. And do keep up the good work. So we're agreed, you can have the sets delivered and set up in time for our rehearsal on April ninth?"

"Your wish is our command," Daddy said.

"But, Regina," Hildie whined, "I thought we agreed we would—"

"This is my show, Hildie, and these men are doing a magnificent job. They're ahead of schedule. Why on earth would I mess with that? I need you worrying more about costumes." She turned to Bunny. "You don't have a grandmother who sews, do you?" Then she laughed.

Bunny wasn't sure if she should join in the merriment. Hildie looked like she might explode. "Uh, no."

"I'm just kidding," Ms. Steffler said. "But not kidding when I ask: do you need anything from me?"

Bunny shook her head. "Not that I can think of at the moment, anyway."

"Well, call me anytime if you do." She slipped her black leather gloves back on and looked out to the driveway. "Hildie, you're blocking my car. Would you let me out? I need to get back to the school and speak to the cast before Mr. Phelps releases them from tonight's singing rehearsal."

She strode away, Hildie following like a bewildered puppy. At her own car, Steffler stopped and turned to add, "And Mrs. Bergen, please send my regards to Mr. Kilbourn, and tell him I hope his father feels better soon."

Well, Regina Steffler was still calling her Mrs. instead of Ms., but given the teacher's turn of humor, she'd gladly let it go.

So the night started out wonderfully, was horribly shaky in the middle, but ended with a stunning triumph. At thirty-nine years old, Bunny Bergen had finally figured out how to stand up for herself. And boy, did it feel good.

CHAPTER TWENTY-SIX

ATE LOOKED AT SAMUEL. EXHAUSTED by the uncomfortable nature of their conversation, he felt the need to lighten the mood. "So, are you a Seahawks fan?"

"Not big into football. The Mariners though—that's another story." Samuel stood, scanning the tabletop around the TV. "In fact, they're playing tonight." He zeroed in on the remote, picked it up and powered on the tube. "How about you? Football or baseball?"

"Baseball. I follow the Nationals."

"The Nationals. Please." Samuel positioned his chair so he could see the television. He clicked the remote until he found the baseball game. "This okay with you?"

Tate raised his beer bottle. "Pizza, Japanese beer, and baseball. An all-American night."

With one eye on the game, they finished off the pizza while talking more sports, movies, and some politics. They kept it light, but learned more about each other.

At midnight, they agreed to call it quits. Samuel had an early flight out, and they both had a long day ahead of them. Tate had a final question that had been nagging at the back of his mind ever since Samuel showed up. He wasn't sure why he cared about the answer, but he did. "So, listen," he said uncomfortably at the door as Samuel was leaving, "what's your plan?"

"In life?" Samuel quipped.

Tate leaned on the door, arms crossed. "You know what I mean. No bullshit."

"Am I here to punish him the way he punished her?"

"Are you?"

"Twenty years ago, I might've said yes. But I'm past it. I've done things I'm not proud of, so why should I throw stones?" He shook his head, staring at the worn rug beneath his shoes. Then he raised his head. "No, man. My plan is to get to know my family again. That's all."

Tate didn't have any experience to judge otherwise, but in his gut, he believed Samuel.

Upon signing the release papers the next day, Tate questioned the admin nurse about the insurance. He'd been burned in the past when one of Morton's doctors claimed a procedure had been approved, but then later the insurance denied the charges.

The short woman scanned the papers through her half-eye reading glasses. She flipped some pages back and forth and made clicking noises once or twice. Finally, she looked up at Tate. "I'm not insurance—that's on the third floor—but looks like everything is being billed to a private party, not Medicare or a major medical insurance of any kind."

"Private party?"

"Mm-hmm." She pointed to the bottom of the form in front of her. "Samuel Alice. Seattle, Washington. Credit card on file."

Tate arrived at Morton's house just thirty minutes before the medical transport ambulance. There was just enough time to get the keys back from Samuel and thank him for getting things ready. The two of them stood for a few awkward moments in the kitchen of the house where they both grew up.

"I'll be at The Monument Hotel. Maybe tomorrow is a better time to make my official appearance, if you will."

Tate nodded. "Let him get settled today. Tomorrow afternoon?"

"May said she'd be here with me."

"Probably a good idea." He opened the refrigerator and saw Samuel had stocked it with the essentials like Tate had asked. Milk, orange juice, eggs, butterscotch pudding, Granny Smith apples, and both vanilla and blueberry yogurt just to be safe.

Tate closed the refrigerator door. "Not that I'm trying to get rid of you or anything, but you're the big boss. Aren't you needed back at the home office or wherever?"

"Tuesday," Samuel said. "I fly out Monday evening."

Tate felt like he should bring up the medical expenses, but Samuel hadn't said anything. He probably wanted it left unspoken. "See you tomorrow, then."

Halfway to the door, Samuel stopped. "I checked—the Nats play at seven tonight. Any interest in catching it together?"

Tate didn't really want to say no, but he had other ideas. "You know," he said, "rain check on that. I haven't even been to my own house, and I wanted to spend some time with Willow..." The man was leaving town on Monday. There was no rain check.

"Sure," Samuel nodded and pulled the front door open. "I understand. See you tomorrow."

The nurse arrived not long after Morton had been made comfortable in his room in his new fully adjustable bed. As she explained the services she would be providing for his father, it became apparent to Tate that this wasn't ordinary hospice.

"Hospice?" she said. "No. This is full-time nursing from The Personal Touch Home Care." She handed him a sheet of paper. "Here are contact numbers for the main office, the local Rustic Woods office, my cell phone number, my supervisor's phone number, and Rustic Woods Hospital. A copy of this has been give to..." she looked down at her clipboard, "Samuel Alice and May Kilbourn."

The nurse seemed to misread Tate's silence for upset. She patted him on the shoulder. "It's okay. We're going to take very good care of your father."

Samuel really had taken care of everything. Tate felt a little guilty saying no to watching the Nats game.

With Morton handled, Tate dragged himself back to his place. His plan was to shower, lay his head down for a few minutes to rest, and then call Bunny under the pretense of checking up on the set building. He did want to know how the set was coming along. Maybe he'd offer to take her out to dinner as a thank you, like they'd talked about. Maybe. He wasn't sure.

The shower felt great. So did the pillow.

In fact, the pillow felt so great that he fell fast asleep and didn't wake until the next morning when Willow set a cup of coffee on his bed stand.

She sat on the edge of his bed. "I'm glad you're back. How's Morty?"

He squinted at her through bleary eyes. "What time is it?"

"Seven." She bounced lightly to rouse him. "In the morning."

"Day?"

"Friday. Really? You don't know what day it is?"

He struggled to raise himself on one elbow and reached for the cup of coffee. "Thanks. I need this." Two sips helped his focus. Willow was still in her pajamas and bathrobe. Her hair was suspiciously unkempt. "Why aren't you dressed for school?"

"Can I stay home today?"

"Are you sick?"

"Sick of school."

"Give me a better reason."

"I want to spend time with my favorite dad."

"You favorite dad will be at work. What's the real reason?"

"My days are so long. I'm exhausted. School, homework, rehearsal. Nothing is due in any of my classes today. My civics teacher will be out, and the sub is showing a movie— *Mr. Jones Does Washington.*"

"*Mr. Smith Goes to Washington.* It's a classic, not a porno. And how about this one: *Miss Kilbourn Goes to School.*" He took another sip of coffee, feeling more and more human by the second.

"Pleeease?"

Tate was playing the hard line, but he already knew from mid-term grade reports that Willow was pulling in straight A's. She deserved the break. He just didn't want her to think he was a pushover. He narrowed his eyes at her. "What will you do if you stay home?"

"Rest some. Then I thought I'd go see Morty. Give him some company. You didn't say how he was doing."

"As good as could be expected, I guess. I should give the nurse a call just to see how he did overnight."

Willow bounced some more on the bed. "Guess what?"

"Guessing games at seven in the morning?"

She bounced some more, and Tate realized she was unusually giddy. "Come on," she said, "play along. Don't be so grumpy."

He laughed. "Don't want to be grumpy. Okay. I'll play. What?"

"Charlie asked me to the prom!" She bounced some more, then stood up and danced in a circle before sitting back down on the bed and giving Tate a playful shake. "He asked me!"

Tate was thrown off-guard. He wasn't sure he was ready yet for his daughter to be dating. "When is the prom?"

"April thirtieth. Aunt May said she'd take me dress shopping. Is that okay?"

"Uh, yeah." He rubbed his head. "Sure."

She stood again and planted her hands on her hips. "You don't seem excited."

"Well, probably because he didn't ask me to the prom." He clutched at his heart and made a sad face. "My feelings are hurt."

She smiled and shoved him. He laughed while trying to keep his coffee from spilling.

"Thank you for letting me stay home. You're a good dad." She skipped out of the room.

Fully expecting a hundred or more voicemails and emails to handle, Tate grabbed an apple and headed to work early.

He was almost right. Twenty-three voicemails and eighty-one emails. Spring had sprung. It would take him two or three days to get through them all, especially since he planned on leaving early to be at Morton's when Samuel "returned."

The clock on his computer monitor read four minutes after eight. Bunny would be at her desk in less than an hour. He set himself a goal of handling at least twelve emails in that time.

He'd take a break to say hi and catch up a bit, then have a short meeting with his junior naturalists, and finally come back to his hole of an office and get to some of the voice mails. This was the part of his job he didn't enjoy—paperwork and politics. He'd rather be out in the field, getting dirty, breathing fresh air.

He focused on the email in front of him and worked, enjoying the silence around him, knowing it wouldn't last long, but looking forward to seeing the smile he had missed for days now.

The sound of footsteps on the wood floors outside his office broke him from the trance of staring at his monitor. Men's shoes, not women's. He sneaked a peek at the time—ten after nine—before looking up to see George's thin face in his doorway.

"I'm back, George. You can stop worrying now." Right away, Tate realized something was different about his boss. Was it his hair?

"Not worried at all," the man responded. "How are you? Everything okay?"

Yeah, now that was definitely different. George had never asked how anyone was doing. "Yeah. Fine. Thanks for asking."

"Your father?"

"At home. Resting." It was the man's pants, Tate thought. He was wearing khakis instead of the gray, threadbare, polyester trousers that bagged in the butt. New khakis that fit. And...loafers?

George smiled. Holy crap. George smiled. "Good. Let me know if there's anything I can do for you. Anything at all."

Tate decided he'd stepped into the Twilight Zone. "Sure," he said, trying not to sound suspicious. "Thanks." When the pointy-nosed man disappeared, Tate laughed to himself. George had to be getting laid. His date with Abigail must have gone really well.

He hit send on email number twelve and stood to stretch. Bunny would be at her desk by now, although he was kind of surprised that she didn't at least check to see if he was in.

He tried to appear casual walking down the hall to the reception desk. Calm. Cool. Reserved. But his spirits dropped when he turned the corner and saw the back of Olga's head instead of Bunny's.

"Olga," he said, "where's Bunny?"

She spun around and blinked through her round glasses. "You are back! How is your papa?"

He ran his hands through his hair and tried to smile. "Good. Thanks. Resting." Yada, yada, yada. "Where's Bunny? I uh... needed to ask her about a message she took while I was gone."

"She is out."

He could see that. "Will she be in?"

Olga shrugged. "Maybe yes. Maybe no. You want I should look at this message for you?"

Tate thought he detected a hint of sarcasm in her voice on the word "message." He said he'd wait for Bunny.

CHAPTER TWENTY-SEVEN

BUNNY HUGGED DADDY. WITH HELP from his lawyer friend, Douglas Hobbs had triumphed in obtaining a permanent protection order from Deena Hobbs-Strickland. She had had her own snooty lawyer there attempting to paint Daddy as mentally incompetent, but it was easy to see from the beginning that the judge wasn't impressed with her or her argument.

Only, once Bunny and Daddy were back outside the courthouse, enjoying the warm sun, he threw her for a loop. "Bunny Cakes," he said, "get your sister on the phone and tell her to meet us at that coffee place you like. What's it called?"

"Daddy! Are you serious?"

"Why wouldn't I be serious?"

"The judge ordered her to stay at least one hundred feet from you. Your own daughter wanted to have you committed."

He shrugged as if it didn't matter. "She wanted control. It's her personality. She needs control because she thinks it gives her attention. But she's still my daughter. I'm not going to stop loving her." He pointed to the phone in her hand. "Go ahead. Make the call. That coffee shop. The Bean Joint?"

"The Java Hut." She narrowed her eyes at him, and then handed the phone over. "You want to do this, you make the call. And keep in mind, I need to get back to work, thank you very much."

More than getting back to work, she was hoping to see Tate. She hadn't talked to him since Wednesday, but he had said then that if all went well, he would be back in the office on Friday. Of course, he had also told her that he'd try to call Thursday when his father was settled. When that hadn't happened, she worried that the transport hadn't gone well.

At The Java Hut, waiting for Demon to arrive, Bunny sipped on chamomile tea to calm herself while Daddy practically chugged a Macchiato double-shot. "How's Morton Kilbourn doing?" he asked. "I know him, you know."

"Yes, Daddy, you told me before." In fact, he'd mentioned it several times during the last few days.

"Been years. I don't think I've seen that man since..."

"Since before Deena was a baby. You were golfing chums. You told me that too."

"He wasn't the kind of man equipped to cope, you know, with his wife's death. And definitely not equipped to raise a baby on his own." He shook his head. "It was like watching a train wreck unfold in slow motion." He leaned over the table. "You like this son of his?" He snapped his fingers trying to remember the name.

"Tate?"

Daddy nodded. "Tate. You like him?"

She put her tea cup to her lips and blew on the steaming brew. "Maybe. I don't really know him *that* well. But, yeah." She smiled and then sipped. *Yeah.*

"I'd like to stop by and see Mort. You think that'd be okay?"

Bunny thought that was a really nice idea. "I don't know, but I'll ask." She sucked in a deep breath and rolled her eyes as she caught sight of Demon waddling through the door. "She's here, Daddy. Remember. You asked for this."

Deena stopped just inside the door and stared at them across the coffee shop where they sat at a table next to the window. Daddy flagged her over. "Get over here, Deena." He had to raise his voice to be heard over the din of the coffee klatchers.

She shuffled her feet. "You're not going have me arrested, are you?" Her voice was even louder than Daddy's, but she added a heavy dose of martyr to her tone.

Bunny cringed as every face in the shop turned to look at her and her father.

Bunny whispered through gritted teeth. "Don't have this conversation in front of the world, Daddy. You want to talk to her, go over there and bring her to the table."

"Yeah, yeah," he said, shaking his head. "You're right."

The process of him shuffling to her side, the two of them arguing in very loud whispers and then shuffling and waddling across the room seemed to take centuries.

To avoid the judgmental stares of the other coffee drinkers, Bunny looked out the window, watching people stroll past.

Finally, Daddy and Deena were seated across from her at the table. Deena clutched her fancy leather purse tightly as if some caffeine-crazed criminal might try to snatch it away.

Daddy slapped the table. "Now. On the count of three, all three of us are going to say 'I'm sorry.'"

Bunny was too shocked to utter a word, but Deena unpursed her lips and protested immediately. "I'm sorry for what? For loving my father?"

"Snap it, Deena," Daddy told her. Then he pointed a finger at Bunny. "Don't you fight me either. No arguments, just apologies. We all have something we're sorry for, so let's say it, mean it, and get on with our lives. Family is too important. Your mother'd be ashamed of us right now."

Deena wasn't very good at 'snapping it.' "Well you're the one—"

Daddy shut her down fast. "We will *all* being apologizing. *All*, Deena." He shook a finger at her. "You really love me? Then do this."

Bunny felt like she'd been apologizing to Demon her entire life. She didn't feel any need to do it now. She watched her sister pout, and then felt a twinge of remorse for calling her Demon her whole life. She supposed she could be sorry for that. Still...

Apparently not ready to give up, Daddy kept talking. "Holding onto anger is like grasping a hot coal with the intent of throwing it at someone else. You are the one who gets burned." He smiled. "Buddha said that."

"Buddha?" Deena shouted. "Daddy, you're a Methodist! What's all of this pagan talk?"

"I'll do it," Bunny said. "I'm in. Daddy's right. Life is too short. I'll say it, and..." The next part was harder to say. "I'll mean it."

Deena's lips pursed again. She looked back and forth between Bunny and their father.

Finally, Daddy held up three fingers for Deena to see. "Three syllables sweetheart. 'I'm sorry.' And I'll say it first: I'm sorry."

It took a while, but Deena finally relented, apologies were made, and they all agreed to forget the past and move forward without grudges.

By the time Bunny had drained her cup of tea, Deena had actually laughed a genuine laugh.

Driving back to work, Bunny wondered how long the truce would last, but she decided to be optimistic rather than pessimistic. Daddy was no dummy, though. He loved Deena, but he knew the protection order had sent her a clear message.

She spotted Tate's truck the minute she pulled into the gravel lot. Her stomach did a little flip-flop, and she couldn't suppress a smile. She had to restrain herself to keep from running through the front doors of the Nature Center.

She wanted to appear interested and concerned, but not eager or needy. Calm. Reserved.

"How did it go?" Olga asked when Bunny set her purse on the desk.

"Great. The judge granted the order. Thank you for covering for me." She looked down the hallway to the back offices. "Um, did Tate make it back today?"

"Oh, he make it back, alright. Comes up here every ten minutes pretending like he needs this thing or that thing. Has big story about he needs to ask you about a 'message.'" Olga mimed finger quotes in the air. "He's got the puppy love, alright." She hopped off the chair and shook her head, but then grinned at Bunny. "You both got the puppy love, yes?"

Bunny put an index finger to her lips. "Shhh. Don't tell anyone," she whispered. "I mean, not that there's anything to tell."

"Don't tell anyone? Everyone knows, Bunny. We just all waiting for you two to, you know, get things going." She winked and then scampered silently down the hall in her nurse's shoes.

Bunny fanned her burning face. Had she been that obvious?

After that discussion, there was no way she could waltz into his office to say "hi" because everyone would know she had ulterior motives. Mortified, she snatched her empty water bottle from the desk. She needed a refill badly.

Thankfully, she found Tate in the kitchen pouring a cup of coffee. She needed water, he needed coffee. No office gossip there.

"Hi," she said, her heart pounding. He looked good. A little tired maybe. He had light circles under his dark eyes, but to her, he always looked good. So, so good.

He smiled at her. "Hi. Olga said you were at the courthouse?"

"For Daddy. It's a bit of family drama, but everything worked out surprisingly well." She felt the need to move closer, but couldn't make her feet budge. "How is your dad? Is he back at home now?" She reminded herself that she was here to get water. She stepped to the cooler and started to fill her bottle.

Tate leaned against the counter. "He is." He seemed eager to change the subject. "Hey, so your son and my daughter, huh? I'm not sure I'm happy about this."

Bunny was confused. "Happy about what?"

"Charlie and Willow going to the prom."

"Hmm." She rolled her eyes. "That's the first I've heard about it."

"Sorry, I assumed you knew."

"Oh, I'd find out," she laughed. "The day before. When he needed a tux." Some hair fell in her face and she tucked it behind her ear.

Tate turned his wrist and looked at his watch. "I need to be getting over to Morton's soon."

"Oh." She wanted to ask him more about his father, but he'd made it clear he didn't like to discuss that subject at work. Suddenly, Bunny didn't know what else to say. She panicked until she thought about the play. "The sets are coming along really well, and Ms. Steffler is actually happy. Stop by sometime and see them if you want. We're moving everything to the school theater in another week or so."

"That's right," he said. "I'd like to do that. Are you going to be around tonight?"

She nodded. "I'll be home. They're not working on the sets tonight." Her mouth was dry as a bone, and she really wanted to take a drink of the water, but she feared she'd dribble down her chin. She kept picturing Tate making love to her and remembering the gentle touch of his lips on her neck and...other places.

"But stop by anyway," she said. She wanted him to stop by. If they saw each other alone, they could talk about *the night*. But he might not want to talk about *the night*. Then she'd feel terrible.

For a brief moment, their eyes locked, and although he didn't speak, Bunny felt sure Olga was right.

Abigail walked into the kitchen, humming a little tune. She'd been humming a lot since her date with George. She opened the refrigerator door and peeked in.

"Tate, I forwarded you an email from Rupert Long." She pulled a soda can from the fridge and popped it open. "He and some other Association board members had some concerns about the paths in the North Woods. I don't know why he emailed me—it's your area. Can you handle him?"

Perfect timing, Bunny thought, to make a graceful exit. "I should, uh, get back to the phones." She wanted to send Tate an extra little smile, but didn't dare.

By four o'clock, Bunny was re-hydrated and was reasonably focused on her job. Michael was on her mind though, because it was Friday afternoon. She was surprised that he hadn't called asking to spend the weekend at Richard's.

She fully expected the request, but had decided to take Daddy's advice and not react negatively. He was a teenage boy who needed his father in his life. She would be supportive of that, no matter how much she hated the creep.

She decided to give a quick call home just to check in.

The phone rang five times before Michael picked up. "Yeah?"

"Hi," she said as chipper as she could manage. "Whatcha doing?"

"Nothin'."

She tried to imagine exactly what kind of nothin' he was doing. You can't do 'nothin'. Even if he was sleeping, he was doing something. "I get off in an hour," she said, "and I thought I'd stop by the store. What would you like for dinner?" This was the moment. If he was going to bring up Richard's, it would be now.

"You know what I really want?" he asked.

Crap. Here it comes.

"Your macaroni and cheese," he said. "Not the stuff from the box. That kind you make in the oven. You haven't made that in forever."

"Oh." Bunny thought she might cry. She choked back the emotion, but her voice cracked a little. "Okay. Yeah. You're right. Macaroni and cheese it is."

"Can we have root beer floats, too?"

"Sure. Ice cream and root beer on the shopping list." She decided to see how far she could push his good mood. "Michael, could you do me a favor?"

"What?"

"Put the dishes in the dishwasher away for me."

"Sure, Mom."

"Is Charlie home?" She knew he didn't have rehearsal, so she figured he must be.

"Yeah. I think he's sleeping."

"Good. Dinner for three then. I'll see you soon. Love you."

"Love you, too."

She hung up the phone, a happy mother. Maybe she'd have a whole night with both of her boys. It had been a long time since they'd spent a Friday night as a family. She tapped her finger on the desk, thinking.

She had invited Tate to come see the sets. She sighed and rubbed her temples. Well, if he came by, and she was having family time, she knew which would take priority. True, Tate gave her goosebumps and bellyjumps, but nothing was more important to her than her boys.

CHAPTER TWENTY-EIGHT

Apparently, Tate missed the fun.

Samuel and May were standing beside May's car in the driveway when he pulled up to Morton's house.

"How long did it take him to kick you out?" he asked, slamming his truck door.

Samuel looked at May. "A minute?"

She looked at him like he was crazy. "A minute? Not even close. Twenty seconds, maybe."

Figuring Morton might need some calming down, Tate stepped toward the house. "I should go in and check—"

May shook her head. "Hold on there, cowboy. You're banned too. He just disowned us all except Willow."

"Willow's in there?"

Samuel nodded. "Willow and the nurse."

Tate noticed circles under Samuel's eyes, and now, more than ever, he saw how much his brother resembled their father. "Are you okay?"

His brother folded his arms and leaned on May's car. "I expected it. We gave it a shot, right?"

"He'll calm down and tomorrow—"

"No," Samuel said. "Not tomorrow."

May put an arm around Samuel. "Tate's right. He'll cool down overnight."

Samuel didn't seem convinced. "It was a bad idea."

Tate pulled his cell phone from the clip on his belt.

"What are you doing?" asked May.

"Texting Willow to come out." He tapped away on his phone keyboard. "I'm hungry. Let's table the Morton discussion for now and get to know each other today. Where do we want to go for dinner?"

May had a painting on exhibit at a small gallery in Old Town Alexandria that she wanted to show them, so they went there first and then chose a seafood restaurant just two blocks away.

They ordered fried calamari as an appetizer, Samuel and Tate drank beer, May drank merlot, and Willow had raspberry lemonade.

And they talked. And laughed. Reminisced. Tate's spirit was lighter than it had been in a long, long time. He felt as if a large boulder had been lifted from his chest.

Halfway through dessert, Tate thought about Bunny. He had said that he would try to stop by her house to see the sets. No firm plans had been made. Still, he wanted to call.

He stepped out onto the street for better reception and less scrutiny from his daughter or his siblings.

Bunny answered. "Hello."

"Hi. It's Tate."

"I know," she said. "Caller ID."

"Right. Listen..." For a brief moment, he thought about telling her what had happened. He considered opening up and sharing some of his own family drama. She'd be happy to listen, he was sure. But he couldn't. Something about her scared him. Or maybe he was scared of himself around her. "I'm not going to make it over there tonight after all."

"Is everything okay? It's not your father, is it?"

"No. He's the same." Tate wasn't lying. Morton was the same. "Just things came up."

Tate heard a man yelling in the background, something about annihilation and ammunition. "Everything okay over there?" he joked, assuming her father was killing animated aliens.

She laughed. "Yeah. We're having a family night. Daddy and the boys are teaching me how to play online video games. I'm a lost cause, I'm afraid. My fingers don't move fast enough."

Tate imagined her working a video game controller and smiled. "I'll let you get back to the killing and mayhem."

"Oh, it's mayhem alright," she said. "Quick thing before you go—I don't know if it will help at all, but did you know that Daddy and your father knew each other years ago?"

"No. I had no idea."

"They played golf together. Before your mother got sick. Daddy would like to see your dad—Morton."

"I'm not sure that's a good idea." Tate was being nice. He thought it was a very bad idea, especially after today.

"Think about it. Maybe seeing an old friend would, I don't know, brighten him up a little or something."

"Morton? Bright? You haven't met the man."

"Well, Daddy asked, so I told him I'd try."

"Fair enough. I'll let you know if he seems up for it, how about that? Have a nice night."

"You too."

Tate hung up. She and her dad were something else. Their hearts were in the right place, but in a million years he could never see Morton wanting to see an old golfing buddy.

Back inside, after he sat down, Willow slid him a sneaky grin. "Who were you talking to? Ms. Bergen?"

"Oh!" May's eye lit up and her long earrings jangled as she danced in her chair. "Ms. Bergen? Who is Ms. Bergen? Wait. Bergen..." She leaned closer to Willow. "Isn't that Charlie's last name?"

Willow nodded, and Tate rolled his eyes.

"Brother," Samuel joked. "You're on the witness stand, and I think these two ladies are about to do some cross-examination."

Tate sat back and crossed his arms. "I plead the fifth."

Morton refused to see Samuel on Saturday.

So instead, without Morton, they all went to a Nationals game, ate too many hot dogs, and watched the baseball team lose badly.

That night Tate dreamed of Bunny. In the dream, he had taken Morton to the doctor for some shots, and Bunny was his nurse.

The doctor told Bunny to give Morton the shots, but when the doctor left the room, she said all Morton really needed was to play some video games.

Tate wanted to argue, but he couldn't, because she was just so beautiful, and she seemed so certain the video games would make him better.

She wheeled Morton to a room filled with old men hooting and hollering in front of a giant, wall-sized television, controllers in their gnarled hands.

Then, she pulled Tate aside and started nibbling on his ear and kissing his neck. He moaned and begged her not to stop.

When his eyes opened he was aware that the sun had come up. It didn't take him long to realize that the sun wasn't the only thing that was up.

He took a cold shower and decided to pay Morton a visit.

"Don't bring that man's name up again," Morton said the minute Tate walked into the room. "I don't want to hear it anymore."

Tate wanted to shout at him and ask him who the hell he thought was paying for this twenty-four hour nursing care. Did he really think Medicare was that generous?

He wanted to shake some sense into the old man. Instead, he decided to try the more flies with honey approach. Mort didn't want to see Samuel? Fine. Maybe he would want to see an old friend from the past. "Don't worry, Mort. I'm just here to see if you need anything."

"I don't need anything."

"How are you feeling?"

"No worse. No better. Hanging in there."

"The nurse says you're eating a little better."

"Maybe." He clicked the remote control, watching the TV situated on top of the tall dresser drawers instead of looking at Tate. "Hey," he said, still clicking, "you know what I'd like?"

"What Morton?"

"Papaya. You think you could get me a papaya? Haven't had one in years."

Tate couldn't have walked into a segue better if he'd planned it himself. "A Papaya. I'll try. Hey, speaking something you haven't done in years, I met someone the other day who says he used to golf with you."

"Who's that?" Click, click.

"Douglas Hobbs."

"I remember Doug."

"He says he'd like to see you. Maybe stop by and say hi."

Morton's gaze fell from the television down to the remote in his hands. He stopped clicking, but he didn't answer.

"What do you say?" Tate prodded.

Morton clicked the remote, powering the TV off. "I'm tired. Ask the nurse to come in here on your way out, would ya?"

Tate wondered why he even tried.

He sent the nurse in and dialed Samuel on his way out the front door. "Hey. When do you leave tomorrow?"

There was hesitation in Samuel's voice. "I was just getting ready to call you. I'm heading back today. Business to handle."

Tate didn't expect that answer. He was going to suggest a hike in Great Falls. The cool March air was fresh, crisp, and invigorating. It was a perfect day for hiking. Tate found that he couldn't manage a response.

"I'll keep in touch though," Samuel said. "And you do the same. Let me know how he's doing."

Tate felt like he should ask if Samuel had plans to return when Morton inevitably took a turn for the worse, but he didn't. They all knew Morton's prognosis: he might survive another week, a few weeks or maybe even a few months. If Morton didn't want to see Samuel now, was he really likely to have a change of heart at the very end? So, all he said was, "Sounds good."

"You and Willow and May should come out to Seattle sometime."

"Yeah. Sure." Tate wondered if they were just exchanging pleasantries now. The words might make them feel better at the moment, but as time passed on, they could easily become just that—words. He plowed ahead because...because he wanted Samuel in his life. "Morton will be buried next to Mom in North Carolina. Just family attending. It's already been discussed."

Silence.

He pressed. He wouldn't chicken out this time. "Please come."

"I will," his brother said. "I will."

He was halfway back to his house when his cell phone rang.

Someone had viewed Morton's condo at Whispering Pines and put in an offer for the asking price. It would be a cash sale. The buyers were ready to sign papers as soon as possible.

So much for a relaxing Sunday.

Tate had half wondered if he'd run into Bunny or her father at Whispering Pines. He never did, despite the fact that he was there off and on throughout the day and into early evening tying up loose ends.

The buyer wanted paint touch ups and new faucets on both the kitchen and bathroom sinks. The closing was set for late the next week, but he wanted to get everything done while he knew he had the time. It gave him plenty of time to think.

By Monday morning, he'd decided his draw to Bunny was as strong as his need to keep her at a distance. The day-to-day uncertainty of Morton's health was already enough for him to handle. Add in the fact that he and Bunny worked together and the situation was even more problematic. The complications were becoming more and more of a burden.

He didn't need the world knowing his personal business. He'd pull back, and let things cool off. He could be friendly, but nothing more, because frankly, she deserved way more than he could give.

Tate reverted back to his old ways and entered the Nature Center from the rear, rather than the front door. He'd been gone nearly a week so there was plenty of work to keep him busy and away from the front desk.

As soon as Lydia and Ross arrived at nine, he called them into his office for a meeting to make sure they were all on the same page with regards to spring events around Rustic Woods.

He kept them talking for two hours with the door closed. By the end, Lydia and Ross were exchanging glances, and he knew he'd taken the avoidance game too far. His meetings never ran over twenty minutes. They were smart naturalists, knew their jobs and did them without much supervision from him. He released them, and they left his office whispering something he couldn't hear. They were probably questioning his sanity.

Avoiding Bunny entirely was impossible. He decided to get a cup of coffee, make a quick appearance with a smile on his face—*see, things are fine and normal and no, my stomach doesn't jump into my throat when I see Bunny Bergen*—then head back to his office to finish the voice and emails lingering from the previous week.

Things might have gone just about that way if his cell phone hadn't rung. It was Morton's day nurse. Morton had a question. "A question?" Tate asked her. "Is that what he said?"

"Not exactly. But he wanted me to get you on the phone."

"Okay." Tate pinched the bridge of his nose between his eyes. He felt a headache coming on. "Thanks. You can put him on."

A moment later Morton's voice, sounding a little weaker than the day before, asked, "Is that you?"

"It's Tate, Mort. Are you feeling okay?"

In the usual Morton manner, he didn't answer the question. "Doug Hobbs," he said instead. "Tell him yes."

"You mean, you want him to visit?"

"Sure." Morton coughed hard into the phone. The cough sounded painful. When he finally caught his breath, he said, "Tell him yes. Come for a visit."

After hanging up, Tate resisted the overwhelming urge to throw his phone across the room.

Instead, he sucked in a deep breath. It appeared that he would be talking to Bunny after all.

CHAPTER TWENTY-NINE

ITTING IN HER CAR WAITING for a red light to change, Bunny wondered if Tate was behaving strangely, or if it was just her insecure imagination working overtime. She tapped the steering wheel with her thumbs as she stared through the sunglasses that shielded her eyes from the late afternoon sun. The days were getting longer. That usually put a smile on her face, but she have one now. Despite the fact that Tate had sought her out to ask if Daddy was available, something about his manner was different. He'd seemed aloof or distracted maybe.

Daddy sat next to her, turning the radio tuner. Static plucked at her nerves until a station came in clearly. Bunny recognized the song immediately: "More Than Words." It was the song she and Tate had danced to at the prom years ago. Hearing it now made her uncomfortable.

"Not that station, Daddy, please." The light turned green, and she concentrated on turning the corner.

"I'm looking for that oldies station," he said. "Where is it?"

She pointed to a set of buttons under the radio tuner. "It's a preset. The second button."

The song grated on her nerves worse than the static had, and she wished he'd press the stupid preset button already. She would have done it herself, but her eyes were busy looking for Morton Kilbourn's street, Wild Cherry Terrace.

Rustic Woods might have been a suburb in a bustling and sprawling metropolitan area, but it had a small town personality. People who moved to Rustic Woods often spent the rest of their lives there. Her best friend in high school, Anna Lutz, had lived on Wild Cherry Terrace, just six houses away from the Kilbourns. Anna's parents still lived on Wild Cherry Terrace, and Anna lived on the north side of town and taught at the elementary school.

Bunny had also babysat for the Websters who lived on Wild Cherry Terrace. Both of those kids were grown now and still lived in Rustic Woods. She'd seen the youngest, Brittney, just the other day at the grocery store with a baby girl of her own.

So when Tate tried to give her his father's address, she was able to say, "That's alright, I remember where he lives."

Pulling into the driveway next to Tate's truck, Bunny was surprised at how run-down the house had become. It stuck out like a sore thumb along Wild Cherry Terrace. The garage door had two cracked window panes, the concrete walkway to the front door was crumbling apart, and the wood siding was in desperate need of painting or complete replacement.

A nurse in scrubs answered the door when they rang, and Bunny's heart sank just a little bit. She had been hoping Tate would greet them. "I'm Bunny Bergen," she said, "and this is my father Doug Hobbs. We're here to see Mr. Kilbourn?"

"Mort," Daddy added.

The woman let them in, and they followed as she walked them through the living room and down a long hall to a first floor bedroom that seemed to be nearly consumed with the hospital bed.

The bed was half-raised, supporting a frail man with thin, white hair and an oxygen tube under his nose. He didn't crack a smile, but raised his hand just enough to acknowledge their arrival. "Doug," he said. "You haven't changed a bit."

Daddy shuffled to Morton's bedside and patted his arm lightly. "You either. I see you're still up to your old tricks, making everyone wait on you hand and foot, right?"

Morton coughed, but didn't reply.

"Mort," Daddy said, "this is my daughter, Bunny."

Bunny stood in the door way feeling very awkward. The little room was too small for the three of them and when the nurse showed up again with a chair for Daddy, she had to squeeze against the door jam to make way. She gave him a little wave though. "Hi, there Mr. Kilbourn. Nice to meet you."

The man raised his hand again. "Pleasure," he said to her. "Sit, Doug, sit."

Daddy sat in the folding chair, and Bunny decided she should let the men do their talking. "I think I'll get our of your way," she said. "Is Tate around?"

The nurse answered Bunny on her way back down the hall. "He's out in the backyard chopping up a fallen tree."

The sun had dipped just below the tree line as Bunny crossed the soft ground, her small heels sinking with each step. She wasn't paying much attention to the ground or her heels though. Tate had most of her attention. Actually, Tate had all of her attention. A white t-shirt hugged his biceps as he gripped an axe, bringing it down hard onto the large fallen tree. Dirty and sweaty, the man still made her go all woozy inside.

"You should be wearing safety goggles," she said, staying far enough away to avoid the flying wood chips.

He squinted one eye at her, then wiped sweat from his face with his t-shirt sleeve. "Yeah. I know."

"What happened here?" She immediately regretted the ridiculous question. *A tree fell, Bunny. Duh.*

"Tree fell last night."

She nodded. "It's a big tree." She bit her lip. She sounded so stupid.

"Yeah."

She nodded some more. "Lot of chopping." *World, meet Bunny Bergen, Master Conversationalist.*

"Yeah." He opened and closed his hand a couple of times. "Your dad is in with Mort?"

Beginning to feel like a bobble head, she forced herself to stop the incessant nodding. "He is. They're talking. So far so good." Darn, she nodded again. "Is your brother still here?"

Tate gripped the ax firmly, raised it over his head and brought it down with intense force. Bunny didn't see how, even with those marvelous muscles, that Tate was ever going to make a reasonable dent in the huge tree with a simple ax.

"He left yesterday," Tate said, wiping more sweat from his forehead. He examined the work in front of him, rather than look her way.

"Oh." Now Bunny knew she hadn't been imagining his aloofness. Tate hadn't said anything about his brother except that they hadn't seen each other in several years, but she suspected that his current mood was related somehow. "Is that a good thing or a bad thing? That he left, I mean."

"I don't know." He squinted at the tree, then pushed at it with his foot. The thing didn't budge.

"I'm sorry," she said.

"Sorry for what?" Tate didn't wait for an answer before taking another chop at the tree trunk. Wood chips flew several feet in all directions. He'd thrown a lot of energy into that one. The ax sliced in deeply.

As he tugged the ax loose, Bunny answered. "I don't know. You just seem upset. I'm sure this is a really hard time for you and your family."

Tate stopped to finally look at Bunny. "I'm not trying to be rude, but I wanted to make some headway on this thing before I lose the light."

Her face flushed. She'd gone too far. "Sure." She nodded again, but didn't care. She just wanted to go hide in the house. "I understand." She turned and made several strides across the yard, but decided to make one more offer. It was the woman and the mother in her.

She turned to face him again. "Let's be honest. You're never going to chop that tree up with a stupid ax. It took three men with chain saws to take apart one in my yard that was half that size. I'm sure it just feels good to hit something right now, but if you feel like talking instead, I'm a good listener."

In response, Tate turned his gaze back to the tree and lifted the ax again, bringing it down fast and hard.

Bunny returned to the house and sat uncomfortably on the worn living room couch. It was a sad room. A small shaft of light crept through between a pair of curtains that were partially open, but the light wasn't enough to brighten the place. There were no pictures of kids on the walls; no prized pieces of handmade art from school years past; nothing that said a family had ever thrived there. *Sorry for what?* he had asked her? *Sorry for this.*

She heard laughter from the bedroom and felt glad that something around the gloomy old house could make her smile. Shifting to cross her legs, her heart raced a little at the sound of a door opening and footsteps she knew were Tate's.

He appeared around a corner and leaned against the wall. His deep brown eyes made her melt inside. Outside, his expression had been hard, tight, and determined, but now it had softened. He looked down at his hand. "You're right about the tree. And the stupid ax."

"Did you get a blister?"

He held up the hand to show her. "Three." He smiled. "Guess I should get the number for those tree guys of yours."

Bunny turned her head at the sound of Daddy's voice in the hallway.

"Get some rest, Mort. Good to see you." Daddy shuffled toward them and offered Tate his hand. "You must be Tate."

Bunny watched as the two men shook hands.

"Thank you for coming, Mr. Hobbs," Tate said.

"Call me Doug. And I'd like to come again. He said he likes the company."

Bunny watched Tate's face for a reaction, but there was none. She rose from the couch and jangled her car keys.

"We should leave and get out of their way and back home, Daddy. The crew will be there soon ready to work." She opened the front door for him and turned to Tate. "See you at work tomorrow, I guess."

He offered her a nod as she stepped out.

"Doug," he said to Daddy, "I want to thank you for helping Bunny take over the set building project for the play."

"Glad to do it. Enjoying the heck out of myself, I have to admit. We'll have them done soon and moved to the school." Then he shook a finger, remembering something. "Speaking of the play, who is the girl Mort talked about? Is that your daughter?"

A deep crease formed between Tate's brows. "Willow is my daughter. Did he talk about her?"

"He said he's not going anywhere until he sees 'the girl' sing in the play. Seems to mean a lot to him."

"Mr. Kilbourn," the nurse said from the hallway, "your father asked for you."

Tate turned. "Tell him I'll be right there."

"Have a good night," Bunny said, giving a little wave. She wished that instead of a wave, she could have hugged him tightly and offered him love, warmth, and understanding. He seemed to need it so badly. "Call me," she said to him. "If you want to talk or anything."

On the drive back to her house, she asked Daddy what the two men had talked about.

"Golf. He asked me if I still played."

"Anything else?" She was curious about Tate's dad.

Daddy shrugged. "Nothing really important. I tried to keep it light."

She shook her head while watching the road. "Families are tricky things, aren't they, Daddy?"

"That they are, Bunny Cakes. That they are."

At home, Bunny quickly chowed down some left-over macaroni and cheese before heading over to the high school. Ms Steffler had summoned her via an urgent text.

It appeared that Hildie Page had just resigned as volunteer coordinator, and Ms. Steffler was desperate for someone organized to step in and take over during the crucial last couple of weeks.

"I thought of you first, Ms. Bergen," Ms. Steffler said. "Tell me you will agree."

Bunny noticed that Steffler hadn't exactly asked, but she had called her Ms. Bergen instead of Mrs., so Bunny was pleased. She was also flattered and not about to turn down the chance to prove to the Rustic Woods community that she was both smart and competent. "Yes," said Bunny, "I'll be glad to take over."

She smiled the entire way home.

When she pulled into her driveway, the garage door was open and kids from the crew were scattered about, working hard. Daddy and Harry stood in one corner discussing a large piece of the set. Harry pointed and Daddy nodded. It looked like an important decision was being made.

She turned off the ignition and was about to open her car door when she noticed an unmistakably familiar dark head of hair. Tate was working a screw driver into something at the far back of her garage. She'd seen a truck parked on the street when she returned, but in the dark, hadn't recognize it as Tate's.

He pulled back to inspect his work, and then turned his gaze in her direction. To her surprise and relief, he smiled. That was a nice change from earlier. She returned the smile and waved through the windshield before slipping out of her front seat.

He made his way through the maze of set pieces and people. The April night was surprisingly warm so she knew it wasn't cool air causing goosebumps to sprout on her arms.

"I came over to say thank you, and they put me to work," he said, using a rag to wipe some dust from his neck. He pointed to the For Sale sign in her yard. "You're selling?"

She sighed. "I can't afford the mortgage. I wanted to wait until the play was over, but my agent said the sooner the better to catch spring buyers. I'm hoping to buy a condo or townhouse near the Nature Center." She cocked her head, still wondering about the reason he gave for stopping by. "Thank you for what?"

"To you and your father." He shook out the rag. "I won't say the visit cheered Morton up exactly, since he hasn't had a cheerful day since I've known him."

Bunny thought is was so strange that Tate how talked about his own father. His words made it seem as if they were acquaintances rather than father and son.

"But," he continued, "he seems to be feeling better."

"That's good. I'm glad."

"And he asked to see Samuel."

This took her a bit by surprise. "They didn't see each other when your brother was in town?"

Tate shook his head. He looked almost embarrassed. "They haven't talked in over thirty years."

Bunny thought about Tate's mood and the tree chopping. It was starting to make sense. "That's terrible."

Four boys from the crew waved at Bunny on their way out. "We have to go Ms. Bergen. See you Thursday."

Bunny waved back and at the same time, noticed Tate's muscles tense.

"I should go too," he said.

She touched his arm. "Stay. I have wine in the house. I'd like to hear about your brother."

"Thanks." He pulled his arm away. "But I have things to do."

He raised his hand to catch Daddy's attention. "I'm heading out, Doug!"

"Catcha later, Tate!" Daddy shouted.

Before Bunny could object further, Tate was leaving. As she watched him walk away from her, she realized that she didn't have a silly high school crush on Tate Kilbourn anymore. She wasn't just feeling the after glow of a satisfying one-night-stand. She had fallen in love with him. Horribly so. Every time she thought about him, every time she saw him, every time she was near him, her longing increased. And darn it, life was short. She was going make something happen, because she had the feeling that he needed her just as badly as she wanted him.

The next several days were very busy for Bunny, but she never stopped thinking about Tate.

He was either very busy himself or doing an excellent job of avoiding her. He managed to be out in the field by the time she arrived at the Nature Center each morning, but Lydia and Ross were also already out. It was springtime in Rustic Woods—the naturalists had a lot to do.

After work, she was either at the high school helping Ms. Steffler or in her garage making the final arrangements for moving the sets to the stage.

She'd managed to corner Tate long enough to arrange another visit between their two fathers. "So, is your brother back?" she asked him. "Did they finally talk?"

"Not yet. He's making arrangements to be away from work for a while, and he'll come a couple of days before the play opens so he can see Willow perform."

"Can I do anything to help?"

He just shook his head. It seemed he'd gone moody again.

When she brought Daddy by the house to see Mr. Kilbourn, Tate was nowhere to be found.

Just a few days before opening night of *Kiss Me, Kate*, Mr. Kilbourn's nurse called the Nature Center looking for Tate. He wasn't answering his cell phone, and to reach Tate before he left work. "His father wants papaya," the nurse said. "He's pretty adamant that he'd been promised papaya."

Bunny could hear frustration in her voice.

Ordinarily, Bunny would have written the message down and put it on Tate's desk, but she decided this was a way she could help. Everyone wanted help, she thought, they just felt guilty taking it when it was offered. She'd skip the offering part and get right on with the helping.

At five o'clock she drove straight to her favorite grocery store for fresh produce. They had ripe papayas just as she expected they would. She bought three of them, along with a bouquet of daisies.

The nurse seemed surprised when Bunny showed up at the door, but smiled when she held up the bag of fruit.

Bunny searched through cupboards in the kitchen until she found an elegant emerald green vase that was just perfect for the daisies. It was covered in dust and cobwebs, but nothing some soap, water, and a little elbow grease couldn't handle.

Pleased with her find, she made her way to the back room. "Hi there, Mr. Kilbourn," she said. "I brought you flowers and papayas, just as the doctor ordered."

Tate's father looked pretty much the same as the last time she'd seen him, although he wasn't wearing the oxygen tubing. His bed was partially raised. The man frowned at her. "Flowers?" he asked. "I didn't ask for flowers."

"I know, but I thought they'd brighten up your room." She set the vase on his chest of drawers. "See, aren't they nice?"

His frown relaxed slightly. "Where'd you find that old vase?"

"Way in the back of the cupboard over your stove. I think it's gorgeous. Green is my favorite color."

"Alice's too," he said. "That vase belonged to her grandmother."

"Alice was your wife?"

He nodded.

The nurse walked in with plateful of sliced papaya. She handed him the plate, raised the bed some more, and fluffed the pillow for him before leaving.

"I'd like to see a picture of her," Bunny said.

"Of Alice?"

"Yes. Do you have one?"

She watched him as he struggled to pick up a slice of the juicy fruit with his frail, shaky hands. "Let me help you," she said reaching toward him.

"I don't need any help! I'm dying, but I'm not an invalid yet." He gave up on the papaya and pointed out the door. "Closet. In the hallway," he said. "You want pictures, there's albums full."

"Should I get them?"

He bugged out his eyes at her. "You're the one that said you wanted to see a damn picture. You wanna see one or not?"

He was right, the closet was full of photo albums stacked on the floor. She counted fifteen of them labeled with dates on the spine, going all the way back to 1956.

She took three from the top and returned to Mr. Kilbourn's room, taking the seat next to his bed. Mr. Kilbourn had finally managed to eat some of the papaya and was wiping juice from his chin.

Bunny opened the album dated 1969 to 1971.

"Scoot a little this way so I can see," Mr. Kilbourn said.

She didn't realize that he had planned on looking at the photos with her. The hospital bed was quite a bit higher than her chair, so she stood so they could easily look together.

"There," he said, pointing a thin finger. "That's Alice."

Bunny looked closer and smiled. Tate had his mother's same dark eyes and brown, wavy hair. In the slightly faded color photograph, a young Alice Kilbourn stood smiling in a flowery bikini, both of her arms wrapped around a child on either side of her. They were on a sandy beach and waves crashed in the background. "Is that May and Samuel?" she asked.

"Uh-huh. That's them. May and Sammy. Alice called him Sammy, I didn't. Makes a boy soft to call 'em baby names, but you can't ever tell Alice what to do."

Bunny noticed that he referred to her in the present tense. She turned the page and looked at more pictures of them on the beach. Tate's mother wore a broad and happy smile in each one.

Mr. Kilbourn pointed to a picture near her thumb in the far right corner. "She liked to make goofy faces."

Bunny laughed. "She was funny?"

"She thought she was."

"Did you?"

He frowned again. "Did I what?"

"Think she was funny?"

He shrugged. "She could make me laugh. She was a good woman. She didn't deserve me, that's for sure."

Bunny heard a door open and Tate's voice call out. "Hello? Bunny?"

"I'm back here!" She flipped another page, scanning the pictures, glad to get a glimpse of Tate's family.

When he appeared in the doorway, she lifted her gaze from the page to look at him and smile.

He didn't return the smile. "What are you doing here?"

"I brought your dad some papaya. They couldn't reach you so—"

"What are you doing with those?" His eyes were focused on the photo albums.

"I asked to see a picture of your mother."

"The papaya was good," Mr. Kilbourn said. "You should find out where she gets it. She must shop at a better grocery store than you do."

"Can I talk to you outside?" Tate's voice had that same rigid tone as the day he'd been chopping the tree.

"Sure. Is everything okay?" She set the photo albums down on the chair and followed Tate down the hall and onto the front stoop. He wasn't kidding when he said outside.

"Boy, you walk fast," she started to quip. When she caught up with him though, and he closed the door behind her, she stopped kidding around. He was angry. "What's wrong?" she asked.

"I didn't ask you to come here today, and I sure as hell didn't ask you to start snooping around in my life."

"Snooping around in your life? I just asked to see a picture. He told me to get the albums out, which, by the way, he seemed to be enjoying. You make it sound like some covert conspiracy."

"There's a lot you don't know about my family."

"I'd like to know more."

"This isn't the kind of thing where you can just sprinkle your magic Bunny dust over and make it all better."

"Are you mad at me or your father? Because it sounds like—"

"I'm not mad, I just want you to go. I'm not a talker, I'm not going to share my feelings with you, and I'm not going to share my life with you, okay?"

Bunny felt the ground sway beneath her feet. Her lungs hurt as if someone had knocked the wind out of her. Even the many hateful words her ex-husband had flung at her over the years didn't hurt her as badly as Tate's words just now.

Unable to utter another syllable, she turned and walked to her car, thankful she hadn't left her keys in Mr. Kilbourn's room.

She couldn't bear to look Tate in the face again.

CHAPTER THIRTY

TATE HAD BEEN ABLE TO avoid Bunny at work, but, as he stood in front of the mirror tying his tie on opening night, he worried that running into her was inevitable. Steffler had reserved seats at the front for family members of the cast and crew. He could have opted to sit in the rear of the auditorium with Morton next to his handicapped seat, but Samuel had offered to sit there, and of course, Tate wanted to be as close to the stage as possible to see Willow.

He was so proud of her. He reminded himself that tonight was about Willow, not about Bunny or his irrational outburst.

Willow was growing up too fast. Tonight she'd sing and act on stage in front of an auditorium full of strangers. When he dropped her off at the school just an hour earlier, she'd been so calm and collected. Not nervous in the least.

In a few days she'd be attending her first prom. He felt like he'd blink, and she'd be graduating and leaving him for college.

Damn. He wasn't getting this tie knot right. He wore one so rarely anymore.

He found May in his kitchen sipping a glass of wine. "Can you fix this for me? I'm hopeless."

"I've been saying that about you for a long time now," she joked, setting the glass down and working the knot with her fingers. "Mort keeps asking about a woman named Bunny. He wants to know if she'll be at the play tonight. Who's he talking about?"

Tate tried to say her name without emotion. "Bunny Bergen."

She narrowed one eye, but kept fiddling with the knot. "Charlie's mom."

"Right. Her dad and Mort were friends. He comes by and visits with Mort now."

"Well, I'm not sure about a grown woman who allows herself to be called Bunny, but you and her: you're a little more than friends?"

He looked over May's head to avoid letting her read his eyes. "No."

"I'm sensing a yes under that no."

"Are you done with the tie and the interrogation?"

"Touchy, touchy, touchy." She finished, patted the knot, and then slapped his cheek.

"What's that for?"

"I knew something was up with you. It's this woman, isn't it?"

"Something is up with me? Yeah, Morton is up with me. In case you haven't noticed, he's been a handful. And it's a busy time at work. And this play."

"Blah, blah, blah," she said. "There's always an excuse."

Tate looked at his watch. "Samuel will be here any minute. I need to get my camera."

She grinned and picked up her wine glass again. "I'll be looking for her. Is she pretty?"

"Drop it, May. Just drop it."

"You have been so cranky lately, little brother. I think you need to get laid."

"Not the conversation I want to have with my sister."

Tate grabbed his camera from his dresser top just as the doorbell rang.

A young girl in a white shirt and black pants handed Tate and May program booklets and pointed them through the double doors into the theater auditorium. Samuel followed them, pushing Morton in his wheelchair.

Tate didn't want to see Bunny, but found himself looking for her anyway. He spotted the reserved seats near the center front. "Down there," he said to May. "That's where we're supposed to sit."

Samuel was already positioning Morton's chair into the handicapped spot on the aisle. "I'll stay here."

"Is Doug here?" Morton asked, coughing just a little.

Doug would be with Bunny. Tate was forced to look for them. He did a quick, nervous scan. "Uh, no, Mort," he said. "Not yet."

"Tell Doug where I am, when you see him. And Bunny too. Tell 'em I want to say hi."

Tate tried to control his irritation. He couldn't believe that when Morton finally chose to get chummy with someone, it was the one person Tate was ashamed see again. "Will do, Mort. May and I are going to take our seats down front."

White sheets of paper with names in black block print were taped to each reserved seat. When he found his name and May's, Tate did a quick glance over the other chairs in search of Bunny's name. He spotted it three rows down. She and her father had earned front row seats.

They sat and May began talking about Samuel and Morton. She'd been stunned, not only by their father's sudden willingness to see Samuel, but also to allow him into his life again. Tate didn't have the guts to admit to May that Bunny and her father probably deserved the credit for Morton's change of heart.

He winced, remembering his rant about magic Bunny dust. She'd looked as if he'd driven a blade through her gut. The reality was that she *had* brought magic into their lives. Into his life. He was fool, and he knew it. A stupid, stupid fool.

Something about seeing Morton and Bunny with those photo albums had set him off. Morton had been willing to share them to Bunny, someone he barely knew, but not share them with his own son.

Tate had poured over those photographs a million times or more growing up, hoping in some small way to feel closer to his mother, but not once did Morton ever join him. If he'd ever had a chance with Bunny, he'd killed it that day.

May poked Tate in the arm. "Did you hear me?" she scolded him.

"No. I'm sorry." He tried to concentrate on May.

"Did Willow show you the prom dress?"

"Oh. Yeah." He nodded, slapping the program on his knee. "She did. Pretty."

"Pretty? Bloody stunning is what it is. Willow is going to knock Charlie's socks off."

The seats were filling quickly with people. Tate looked at his watch. The lights would be dimming any minute now. He turned in his seat to see how Samuel was doing, only to catch sight of Olga, Abigail, and George in the center aisle. George waved, but Olga and Abigail weren't so nice. Their glares were venomous. Okay, so Bunny had told them he was an ass. He had that coming.

When he turned back around, he saw her. She'd fixed her hair up into a pretty bun and a few stray wisps fell onto her nearly bare shoulders. He remembered running a finger along those soft, white shoulders not so long ago. He ached to kiss them now.

Their eyes caught for just a moment, but then she pulled her green shawl over her shoulders and turned to take her seat.

Doug waved. "Hey, Tate!" Where's your pop?"

Tate motioned toward the back where his father sat. Doug gave a thumbs-up, and waved to Morton.

The lights dimmed, the orchestra began to play, and Tate sucked in a deep breath.

Willow had the voice of an angel. He was completely captivated every time she was on stage. Several times he thought he'd cry. She inherited her beauty and talent from her mother, and he felt that somehow, Jill was there, watching her and smiling.

When Willow wasn't on stage, his gaze wandered. From where he sat, he could see Bunny's profile. He could watch her smile and laugh.

She disappeared during intermission, which was a relief, but Olga found and pulled him aside.

"Where I come from," she said, looking up at him through her round-framed glasses, "someone like me would put a curse on someone like you." She poked his chest for emphasis.

He didn't have a response.

"Ack," she went on, "not really. We are not so much for the curses, but you," she pointed a stern finger at him, "you are an idiot and deserve to be cursed."

That Olga, always afraid to speak her mind. He excused himself from the verbal whipping to get a drink of water from the fountain. A voice startled him as he drank.

"Tate Kilbourn."

He wiped water from his mouth and turned around to see Colt's friend, Barbara Marr, staring at him. Her curly hair looked a little wild.

Knowing she was Bunny's friend as well, he suspected another lecture was forthcoming. "Hi?"

"Did you know that I shot Bunny in the foot?"

Good Lord, this woman was fruitier than the rumors reported.

"No."

"You should," Barb said. "You should know that. Do you know why I shot her in the foot?"

"Are you serious?"

"To save her life. I didn't save her life so you could stomp all over her heart, I'll tell you that right now." She shoved a piece of paper into Tate's hand. "That's my phone number. If you have half a brain, you'll make it right with her, and I want to help. Colt says you're a good guy, and I trust him, otherwise, I wouldn't be offering."

Tate shook his head. "Okay."

The lights blinked off and on, signaling everyone to return to their seats for the second half.

"Your daughter is very talented, by the way," Barb said smiling, finally.

"I'll tell her you said so."

"And for God's sake," she said, walking away, "ask Bunny about her foot."

He returned to his seat next to May feeling shell-shocked. He looked at the paper in his hands and then at Bunny.

May whispered in his ear. "I've been watching you watching her. I haven't seen that look in your eye since Jill."

The lights dimmed and the orchestra played again.

CHAPTER THIRTY-ONE

THE LATE AFTERNOON SUN WARMED Bunny's face and she was glad for that, but it didn't calm the butterflies that flapped like crazy in her stomach.

According to Charlie, Tate had invited her over to take pictures of the couple before they left for dinner and the prom.

She still wasn't sure. "That's what he said?" she'd asked Charlie. "'Invite her?'"

"Yes, Mom."

"He specifically used the word *invite*?"

"Mom! Just come!"

She considered calling Tate herself to confirm, but the trauma of his blow-up was still fresh in her mind. She'd just go, take a couple of quick pictures of Charlie and Willow, say thank you, and leave. She could do that with grace. At least, she hoped she could.

Her flip-flops slapped against her heels as she walked up the sidewalk that led to the courtyard at the front of Tate's house. The scent of blooming hyacinth tickled her nose just before she heard Willow's sweet laughter.

Tate's back greeted her as she entered the courtyard. He focused his camera on the gorgeous couple. Charlie could have modeled the black tuxedo and bowtie for a magazine; he looked so handsome. The peach-colored rose boutonnière on his lapel matched Willow's strapless, floor-length gown. The simplicity of the tulle on the dress and the tiny beadwork on the bodice illuminated Willow's beauty. Her hair reminded Bunny of the glamour styles from the 1940's. It hung all on one side, falling like a dark, rich waterfall over her right shoulder. The girl's beauty took her breath away. She could only imagine how Charlie felt.

Willow and Charlie smiled for the camera, and after Tate clicked, Charlie gave her a wave. "Come on in, Mom."

Tate spun around. His face lit up with a wide smile. His brown eyes locked on hers. Bunny caught the hint of hesitation in his voice. "Hi."

It was easy to get lost in those eyes, which was why she offered a quick, "hi" before focusing on Charlie and Willow. Nervously, she tucked stray strands of hair behind her ear.

"I'm glad you came," Tate said.

That was good, she thought. He was glad she came. He didn't spit on her or tell her to get her pictures and get out. He was glad she came. She nodded a little, relieved. "How's your father doing? I've been thinking of him."

"You know, he has his good days and his bad days, but he's not as cranky. He and Samuel are actually getting along."

"I'm glad." That annoying hair kept falling in her face. She tucked it behind her ear again. "Well, I guess

I should get snapping, huh?" She took a few steps closer, landing next to Tate, but making sure not to stand too close. Despite her attempts to keep a decent distance, she swore she could still feel warmth radiating from him. She knew it was just her imagination, but she had trouble concentrating anyway.

She lifted her small, digital camera. It paled in comparison to Tate's large, professional looking apparatus. After framing them in the shot and pressing the auto-focus feature, she shouted, "Say cheese doodles!"

Willow's resulting laugh was perfect for Bunny's shot, only nothing happened when she pressed the shutter button. Well, something happened: the camera powered off.

"Noodles!" she swore.

"You mean, doodles?" Tate said, smiling.

Bunny pressed the tiny power button. Nothing. "No, I mean, noodles. My camera shut down." She pressed the power button again. Wait for it. Nothing. Again. Nothing. She felt her face flushing, knowing Tate's eyes were on her, watching her every silly, ridiculous move.

"What's wrong, Mom?" Charlie asked her, his arm still around Willow's waist.

"It shut down, and I can't get it back on."

"Did you charge the battery?"

"Yes, Charlie. I'm not an idiot."

"Do you want me to take a look at it?" Tate asked.

She heaved a sigh. "Sure." As he took it from her, their fingers brushed. Even the tiniest feel of his skin against hers caused a tingle to rippled across every nerve in her body.

She watched as Tate pushed the power button the same way she had, then flip open the battery bay, eject the battery, re-insert, and try the power button again. Her shoulders dropped. She couldn't believe her luck.

"It's dead, alright," Tate said, handing the camera back to Bunny. "But I'll just send you these." Before she knew it, he was next to her, his arm touching hers, and positioning the large display on his own camera for her to see the photographs he had already shot.

They were ten times better than anything she would have managed with her own anyway. Tate pressed an arrow and the stunning pictures scrolled by on the display. Okay, there was one with Charlie's eyes half-closed, but other than that, they were all spectacular. And even more spectacular than the pictures was Tate's breath on her shoulders and in her ear. She felt her knees go a bit weak and her heart rate kick up a notch.

"Those are great," she said. "You're better than some professionals I've seen."

"He's taken tons of photography courses," Willow said.

"Let me take a couple of you and Charlie," Tate suggested.

"No, no," she protested. "This is their day."

Willow stepped away from Charlie. "Great idea! Come here." She waved Bunny over.

Bunny had primped quite a long time before arriving, it was true. She was certainly photo-ready. She just wasn't sure she could look natural with Tate scrutinizing her through his telephoto lens.

Trying to appear relaxed, she patted the sweat from her palms onto her cotton capri pants while stepping up to her handsome son and hooking an arm around his waist. She thanked her lucky stars that the pants were navy blue and wouldn't show the wet spot from her hands. She tried for a natural smile that didn't reveal her nerves.

Tate took shots of them from a couple of different angles. Bunny's cheeks began to cramp. She was greatly relieved when he stopped and Charlie said, "I think we should get going. Our dinner reservations are for six thirty."

Bunny had never heard her son worry about being prompt before, and she imagined he was more interested in being alone with his date. The thought caused her to smile again, and she jumped when the camera flashed.

"Sorry," Tate said, grinning. "Had to catch that smile."

Was he flirting with her?

Willow jumped up on her tip toes to plant a kiss on Tate's cheek. He returned the gesture with a hug. "Have a good time you two. Home by two, right?"

"Right," agreed Charlie.

Bunny and Tate turned at the same time, watching their children walk away. Once they were out of sight, Bunny knew she needed to make her own exit, although she hoped, with the friendly smiles and possible flirtations, that Tate would stop her.

When she turned around to say good-bye, Tate was holding a red rose and looking into her eyes.

"I was an asshole," he said.

She would have said something in return except a lump had materialized in her throat as she fought back tears.

He leaned forward. "That's kind of my way of saying, I'm sorry."

"Okay." Her voice was weak. "I'm sorry too."

"You don't to be sorry for anything. You've been nothing but generous and kind. If I had been outside of myself watching me talking to you like that, I would have punched my lights out."

She laughed. "I'd pay to see that trick."

"I always said I wouldn't be like Morton, but it turns out that I really am. I shut people out."

"I don't think he's a bad person, and I know you aren't."

"I was really hoping you would come tonight. Actually, I planned on it."

"You did?"

"I made dinner. Can you stay?"

Yes, yes, yes! "I suppose." She took the rose from him and sniffed its aroma.

With his large camera still in his left hand, Tate took several long steps to his front door and opened it for her, motioning for her to enter. Even his simple movements sent delightful shivers up and down her arms. She followed his lead and as she passed him, she couldn't help but reach out, squeezing his hand with hers.

So many thoughts went into the single squeeze. She wondered if he understood even a millionth of them.

He returned the squeeze as she entered his house. He closed the door behind her.

"Okay," he said, placing his camera on the credenza near the door. "Wait right here. Just for a minute."

She breathed in the aroma of basil and spices. "Smells amazing. I didn't know you were a cook."

He smiled. "You're smelling one of about two dishes I do well." He put his hands up to motion her to stay put. "Don't move. I'll be right back." Tate slipped through the passageway that led to his dining room while Bunny fiddled nervously with the camera in her hand. She decided to place the broken thing on the credenza next to Tate's as she listened to the sounds of things clinking from the dining room.

Her hands had gone from sweaty to ice cold and her toes were feeling a little icy as well. She was beginning to regret wearing the stylish flip flops.

"Okay," she heard Tate call out. "You can come in!" His tone was uncharacteristically playful.

When she entered the room, her breath stuck somewhere between her lungs and her throat. Tate had dimmed the sconce lights on the wall and lit a pair of tall white candles. The table was set for two and covered in rose petals. The flickering candlelight reflected in Tate's eyes, and if that wasn't enough to melt her heart, the corsage in his hand finished her off.

Taking her hand and pulling her close, he slipped it over and onto her wrist, then gently pulled her hand to his mouth and kissed her palm. "There's more."

Bunny didn't need more. She had all she wanted right there, right now.

Tate pulled a remote from his back pocket, pressed a button, and set it down on the table. He pulled her to him with his hand pressed against the small of her back. He looked into her eyes, assuring her that she was the only one for him in all of the world.

"More Than Words" began to play from speakers somewhere around them. When they had danced to this song at their own prom, Bunny hadn't known if Tate knew her from the piece of gum on his shoe.

Now, so many years later, she was locked in his arms, and his eyes were on her. It wasn't a dream, and it wasn't just a memory anymore either. "You remembered?" she asked.

"You're not an easy person to forget." He moved in a slow rhythm, pressed against her, and she followed. "It feels right, dancing with you again.

"Listen," he said, pulling her hand to his chest, as they swayed gently. "I'm not the most talkative guy, and I don't wear my heart on my sleeve or share things easily. And it's been a long, long time since I've...I mean, since someone has..." he stopped and laughed a little. "I had this rehearsed, you know. Had a little speech all prepared."

She shook her head lightly. "It's okay. I don't need the speech." The feel of his warm breath on her lips made her head light.

"But I need to say it. I am crazy, crazy in love with you. And I *do* want you in my life. Every part of it." His hands tightened on the small of her back, igniting an explosion of desire. "And," he said rubbing her nose with his, "I want to know all about your foot."

She laughed. "What?"

"I want to know why Barbara Marr shot you in the foot," he said.

"Oh. That's a long story."

"We both keep saying that." He stroked the small of her back with his thumb.

"Time to start talking then, I guess, huh?" The gentle sway of their slow dance, and the closeness of their bodies made Bunny ache.

"Yeah," he agreed.

"But before we talk, would you…"

"Would I what?"

"Would you kiss me, Tate?"

"Oh, you did not just say that." He grinned, minimizing what little space remained between their faces.

She laughed again. "I couldn't resist."

"You want a kiss?" he asked. "You mean, like this?" He touched her lips lightly The tease made her shiver. Then he pressed tighter, opening his mouth to taste her more fully, still swaying, moving her body with his, the rhythm of the song guiding them both.

Yes, she thought, *just like that.*

Eventually they would make the time to talk, and they'd learn all they needed to know about each other.

But that kiss…

That kiss told her more than words could ever say.

THE END

ABOUT THE AUTHOR

Karen Cantwell lives and in Virginia just outside of Washington, D.C. When she's not writing or tending to the needs of her wonderful family, she can be found working in her garden or relaxing on the couch watching a favorite classic movie.

Kiss Me, Tate is the first book in the new Love in Rustic Woods Series, a romantic spin-off from her popular Barbara Marr Murder Mysteries.

If you'd like to receive email notifications about future Karen Cantwell releases, please subscribe to her newsletter here. Your email address will *never* be shared or bombarded with frivolous junk. You may unsubscribe any time.

Karen loves to hear from readers! For her email address and to learn more about Karen and her books, find her at KarenCantwell.com.

MORE BOOKS BY KAREN CANTWELL

Would you like to read more about Bunny Bergen and her friend Barbara Marr? Try the Barbara Marr Murder Mystery Series:

Take the Monkeys and Run (A Barbara Marr Murder Mystery #1)
Citizen Insane (A Barbara Marr Murder Mystery #2)
Silenced by the Yams (A Barbara Marr Murder Mystery #3)
Saturday Night Cleaver (A Barbara Marr Murder Mystery #4)
Dead Man Stalking (A Barbara Marr Murder Mystery #5)—Nov. 2013 release

The Chronicles of Marr-nia (Four Barbara Marr Short Stories)
It's a Dunder-Bull Wife (A Barbara Marr Holiday Tale)
Bjorn! on the Fourth of July (A Barbara Marr Short Story)

Keep Me Ghosted (A Sophie Rhodes Ghostly Romance #1)